ALSO BY JAN MARK

Aquarius

HANDLES

Jan Mark

HANDLES

ATHENEUM   NEW YORK
1985

Library of Congress Cataloging in Publication Data

Mark, Jan.   Handles.

SUMMARY: Erica, a lover of motorcycles, finds her
country holiday dreary until she runs into a cat with
false teeth, new friends with interesting names, and a lot
of motorcycles.
1. Children's stories, English. [1. Motorcycles—Fiction. 2. Country life—Fiction] I. Title.
PZ7.M33924Han 1985   [Fic]   84-20467
ISBN 0-689-31140-0

For
Marian Brown

Chapter One

The lady tourist, who had been hovering uncertainly with a map for several minutes, finally said, 'Excuse me, dear; is that the cathedral?'

Erica pointed to the distant spire that rose above the roof-tops.

'No, that's the cathedral. This is St Peter Mancroft.'

Tourists were always making that mistake. The cathedral was down in a hollow, near the river; St Peter Mancroft stood on a hill above the market, across the road from City Hall and quite close to the motor-cycle park, which was where Erica was sitting on the wall that lay alongside the steps leading down into the market place.

The lady tourist had not finished. 'Could you tell me where the Castle is? I think they said there was an art gallery there.'

Erica would not have thought it possible to miss the Castle, which was right in front of them, on a hill of its own, a few hundred metres away. She pointed it out, gave directions, explained patiently that the flint building on the left was the Guildhall and yes, it really was as old as it looked. The lady wandered away with her friends, seeming entirely unconvinced, in the wrong direction, and left Erica on the wall beside the motor cycles.

It was August, and the summer streets of the city had been crowded all day with tourists who could not speak English, or who could speak English but could not read a map, or who could do neither, nor even recognize a castle when they saw one. There was a special exhibition at Norwich Castle this month, but Erica did not intend to go and see it. The only exhibition that interested her was right here, at her feet, in the motor-cycle park. Most of the machines were perfectly ordinary, and many of them turned up day after day, because their owners worked in the city and left them there as other people would park their cars, but sometimes there were rarer specimens to be seen; a Triumph Thunderbird, or a Honda Gold Wing. Erica had never forgotten the day that a stranger had ridden in, like a sinister visored knight, on a Vincent Black Shadow, and once there had been a girl with an Electra Glide, who had simply sat there, in blue leathers, waiting for admirers. Her ambition was to see an Indian, but none had ever turned up. Perhaps no one who actually owned one of the fabulous beasts would dream of leaving it in a public motor-cycle park.

It was getting on for six o'clock now, and one by one the bikes were leaving, roaring away towards Chapelfield or St Giles Street, but not too wildly because the Police Station was just round the corner, stealthily tucked in under the side of City Hall. Even the huge BMW R-100, with a saddle like an armchair and elegant fairings, and which had been there since lunchtime, was finally claimed. There was nothing left worth looking at. Somewhere out near Yarmouth, she had heard, there was a museum, in the grounds of an old castle, where there were galleries lined with ancient, rare, spectacular cars and motor cycles. She had located it on a map, but it did not seem to be anywhere near a bus route, and Mum or Dad would not be interested in driving there. Mr Pearson, from the flat next door, treated his Honda 250 as a valued friend, but it had to earn its keep. He did not care about bikes that had been built decades ago and were kept only for show.

Erica dropped from the wall, a death-defying, bionic plummet onto the steps below, and went down into the market. The stalls were closed and the stall-holders going home. For most people the market ceased to exist once this had happened; they went there only when they could buy something, and had no idea of what a market-place could become when it was emptied of people. It stood on a slope, half a dozen alleys stretching downhill, and as many running across them, endless corners round which to lurk and hide. It was not supposed to be used like this, but neither was the multi-storey car park, which was where Erica went when she was not in the market or hanging about in the yard behind the flats, watching the lads with their bikes and picking up useful scraps of information. When Erica had been small, she had said that she wanted to be a nurse, because that was what everyone else wanted to be, then, and Mum had got it firmly fixed in her mind that this was still what she wanted to be. Nothing that Erica said or did could make her understand that all Erica wanted to be now was a motor-cycle mechanic. There was no point in mentioning it to Dad, either. He would not think it even possible for a woman to become a mechanic; it would be almost as unnatural as men having babies. Erica had not heard him say this, but she knew that it was what he thought. Craig, who was fifteen, really did want to become a nurse, but he too had not said anything to Dad. Erica hardly dared to guess what Dad might say about that, and neither did Craig.

The market was almost deserted by now, and among the few people who still lingered there she saw no one whom she knew. That meant that the Crowd was assembling in the multi-storey car park. No one ever arranged beforehand where to meet, but somehow everyone knew, and eventually everyone arrived. Erica, on the whole, preferred the market; the multi-storey car park always smelled of burned coffee, even after all the cars had gone, and it was not so easy to get out of as the market, with its numerous escape routes. Still, Mum was expecting her home for tea, and she would have to come back through the market to reach the car park. Possibly a stray member or two of the Crowd would be there and they could form a splinter group; although in the Crowd it was not Erica who gave the orders. In fact no one gave orders, but when several people had the same idea at once, Erica was not usually among them.

When she reached the courtyard behind the flats Mr Pearson was just home from work, putting his Honda away in the garage, and two of the Murphys were holding a consultation over a poorly moped, like doctors arguing over a patient. They pretended not to see Erica because they knew that she would make her own diagnosis without being invited to, and that probably she would be right. When this happened the Murphys called it feminine intuition; they could not believe that she might *know* what was wrong. There were four Murphys, all boys.

The flats were only four storeys high, and there was no lift. Erica went up the concrete stairs three at a time, overtaking and passing Michael, the youngest Murphy, on the second flight.

'Show-off!' Michael yelled after her, because he knew he could not catch up with her. 'You can't really run that fast!'

'I suppose you think this is feminine intuition too,' Erica shouted back, her voice echoing round the corner, past Michael and all the way to the bottom of the first flight. She heard it hit the wall and start on its way up again.

The Timperleys' flat was on the third floor. The front door stood on the right of the staircase, with the Murphys opposite and, straight ahead, the Pearsons. Mrs Pearson liked growing things, and suffered from having no garden. Her flat was full of plants, and when one grew too large, she put it outside the door, on the landing. This had been going on for several years now, and the third-floor landing had become a small rain forest of rubber plants, Swiss cheese plants, leggy avocados and a great bush of scented geranium that breathed perfumed gusts if anyone passed by and disturbed the air round it. Sometimes a plant mysteriously died, and Mrs Pearson secretly whispered to Mrs Timperley, who was Erica's mum, that one of the Murphys must have poisoned it, but she never said anything to Mrs Murphy because the landing was small, and peace depended upon everyone remaining friendly; and it was Mrs Murphy who had contributed the strip of red carpet which had been on the stairs when she lived in a house. That and the plants made the third-floor landing look very plush. It reminded Erica of the place outside the head teacher's office at school, that was done up to impress visitors. There was hell to pay if you stood on Sir's bit of carpet with muddy shoes, and nobody poisoned *his* plants, although there were a number of people who would have liked to try.

The front door was on the latch, and Erica stepped into the little square hall to find it full of lanky Craig, standing on a suitcase, while Mum knelt at his feet, trying to close the catches.

'You're not going camping with a *suitcase*, are you?' Erica said. 'I thought you were supposed to have a rucksack and things like that, for camp. Jason'll think you're soft.'

'You be quiet. He won't think anything,' Mum said. 'I can't afford a rucksack specially, not just for one holiday. He might not ever need that again. There's nothing soft about a suitcase. You don't want to go round saying things like that.' Craig was not at all soft, but he was gentle, and people seemed to think that this was almost as bad. Dad, and especially Mum, were always afraid that people would think he really was soft. Erica was sorry that she'd mentioned it, even as a joke.

Craig said, 'Jason'll be here in a few minutes. Hang you out of the window and tell us when he comes.'

Erica stepped round him, and the suitcase, and Mum, and went into the living-room, which looked out over the street. Although the window was opened wide the room was very hot, as it faced south, and Erica was glad to hang out over the sill, sipping at the small breeze that filtered round the corner of the building and could be reached only by laying her face against the brickwork. Craig had been invited to go camping for three weeks with his friend Jason from school and Jason's brother, who was old enough to drive and had borrowed a van from a mate. It was lucky, Erica thought, that Jason's brother was out of work, and so free to take them, or Craig would have had no holiday. Then she remembered that there was nothing lucky about being on the dole, and was glad that she had not said what she was thinking. There really would have been a row then, because there was talk of redundancies at Dad's factory, too. Craig and Jason and the brother were going to the Yorkshire Dales. Erica was not going anywhere.

At the end of the street she saw a dirty white van come slowly round the corner.

'Is that a Transit?' she shouted, over her shoulder. 'VLR 252G?'

'I don't know what the number is,' Craig said, coming into the room behind her. He leaned out of the window. 'Yes, that's it. They're here,' he called to Mum. Then he turned to Erica. 'I'll send you a postcard,' he said. 'That's a pity you can't come too, but Jason'd've gone up the wall if I'd said anything. So would Mum.'

'I don't mind,' Erica lied. She would have given her eye teeth to go, but as she had not expected to be invited she was not precisely disappointed; just sad.

'Well, cheer up anyway,' Craig said, knowing how much she was minding it. 'Mum's got a surprise for you. She'll tell you after I've gone, but don't let on that *I* told you.'

'What is it?'

'No – that's her surprise; she'll tell you presently.'

He went. Erica leaned over the sill and watched until he reappeared, foreshortened in the street below, with the suitcase, still unfastened, wedged shut under his arm, and a carrier bag hooked over his elbow. He really would have looked better with a rucksack. Jason's brother, who had just begun sounding his horn, climbed out of the van to let him in. Craig looked up and waved, then he was out of sight in the van, which reversed onto the pavement, turned and drove away, just as Mum came out too and stood under the window, waving. The van turned right at the end of the street, and he was gone.

Erica stayed at the window and wondered about the surprise. It was only half a surprise now, because she knew it was coming, but she was glad in a way of the warning. There was a chance that it would be a surprise that she did not want, and now she would at least have time to rearrange her face if it turned out bad; she would be ready for it.

She heard Mum's footsteps outside, loud and hollow on the concrete stairs, soft on Mrs Murphy's strip of carpet, and sniffed a strong smell of scented geranium as Mum failed to avoid it as she came through the front door.

'Well,' Mum said, closing the door behind her, 'that's the last of him for three weeks. Now, what about you?'

Here it comes, Erica thought. She said, 'I'm all right. I'm going out down the market, after tea.' She never mentioned the multi-storey car park.

'No, you're not.' Mum smiled. The surprise was about to be revealed. 'You'll be busy.'

Erica played up.

'What doing?'

'Packing,' said Mum. She was beaming, watching Erica at the same time. Erica managed to look tremendously pleased and astonished.

'Packing? What for?'

'You're going on holiday too,' Mum said. 'I didn't tell you before in case that didn't work out, but I had a letter from Joan this morning.'

'Auntie Joan?' Auntie Joan was not someone associated with holidays. She lived out at Calstead, about twenty miles away, on the wrong side of Norwich, as Erica thought of it. Calstead was a very small village, the kind that had to be described in advance and pointed out as you went through, otherwise you missed it. 'What does she want?'

'She wants you to go out there and stay with her and Uncle Peter and Robert for a bit.'

'*Wants* me?' Erica said. Mum looked slightly guilty.

'Well . . . I wrote and asked her if she'd like you to stay for two or three weeks . . . I mean, she's mentioned that often enough, you or Craig going over there, only Craig doesn't get on all that well with Robert . . .'

Robert was their cousin. Erica knew Robert. She felt that he was not the kind of person that anyone could get on with, but she tried to keep her delighted smile in place.

'When am I going?'

'Tomorrow.'

The smile slipped a bit. 'But I'm not ready or anything. Nobody knows I'm going. I can't even say good-bye properly. Can't I go on Thursday?'

'Joan did say tomorrow. I mean, she wrote on Friday, but I suppose she forgot to post that until Saturday and that didn't get collected until yesterday.' In spite of Erica's efforts, Mum looked worried.

'Can't we ring?'

'Joan hasn't got a phone. You know that.'

She wouldn't have. Erica thought of Calstead, and the little house beside the Happing road, among the beet and barley fields, and felt as if she were about to be marooned.

'You do want to go, don't you?'

'Oh *yes*,' Erica said. In a way it was true, but it was becoming less true by the minute. When Craig had hinted that something might be going to happen, she had almost begun to be excited, and if only she could have had a few days' grace she might get properly excited, and pleased about going on holiday, but it was all happening too fast. This time tomorrow she would be in Calstead.

'What'll you do while I'm away?'

'Oh, I'll manage,' Mum said. 'Don't worry.' She saw Erica's sceptical look. 'I'm not trying to get rid of you,' she said, quickly.

14

Up to that moment Erica had not dreamed of thinking such a thing.

'I'm not, really.'

'No,' Erica said.

Chapter Two

Erica could scarcely remember the last time she had been at Calstead, and on that occasion they had arrived in the car. The countryside looked very different from the top of a bus; there was more of it, for a start, and it seemed rather flat after the hills of Norwich. Mum had given her a careful description of what she would see as the bus approached the village, so that she would know where to get off. It was written on a piece of paper, with strict instructions to go down to the lower deck, so as to be ready, when the bus stopped in Polthorpe.

'Suppose that doesn't stop?' Erica had said. This seemed likely already. It was a midweek midday bus, and there were very few people on it, and most of those had left it at Wroxham.

'That always stop in Polthorpe,' Mum had said. 'They change drivers there.' The longest stop that the bus had made so far had been in a village off the main road, where the street was so narrow that the driver had been able to lean out of his window and buy cigarettes from the shop on the other side, without leaving the bus. This seemed to be a routine event, since the woman in the shop had obviously been expecting him, and had had the cigarettes ready.

it the red and white finger of the Happing
light, stu, p from the horizon, to point out where the
sea lay, y a water tower shone white in the sunlight.
On the aw church towers, and on the left, too, but
none of t, n h spires.

'There ne church in Norfolk with a spire,' Mum
often said, 'and that's Norwich Cathedral.' Erica wondered if
she were right, and why she sounded so proud about it. They
never went to church, but if they had done, she supposed, the
cathedral would have been the nearest. St Peter Mancroft had
a kind of lead pinnacle on top of its tower, but that couldn't
be called a spire.

Now there was a road junction, and a sign saying POL-
THORPE, where the road turned left from the by-pass which
went on to Yarmouth. The by-pass was built on the track of
an old railway, and the station was still standing, turned into
offices. As Mum had promised, the bus drove a little way into
Polthorpe and stopped. Erica collected her belongings, all in
carrier bags because Craig had the suitcase, and went downstairs to be ready for the entry into Calstead. According to
plan, the driver shut off the engine and stepped out of the bus.
It stood in the sunshine, smelling hot and oily. Two women
climbed out, but no one boarded it, and the driver stood on
the pavement, smoking one of his cigarettes, chatting to a
friend and keeping a watchful eye on his bus until another
man, in the slate-coloured Eastern Counties uniform, came
unhurriedly up the street to join them. He did not seem too
anxious to begin his shift, and lingered with the first driver and
his friend for a smoke and a chat. Things moved more slowly
here.

At last the second driver climbed in, started the engine, and
the bus moved off. Erica took out her piece of paper again and
began to look out for the landmarks that Mum had recorded
for her.

On the left, at the bottom of Polthorpe Street, a garage: here it
was, and they turned left beside it. *On the left again, Polthorpe*

Comprehensive; they passed that, and the council estate, and were out in the open country once more. Erica was the only person left on the bus. The driver called over his shoulder, 'Where to, love?'

'Calstead Corner,' Erica said. 'By Nudd's Stores.'

She thought that probably the driver would know better than she did where the bus-stop would be, until she noticed that out here there were no bus-stops. Then she hoped he would remember where she was getting off, because even from down here she did not recognize the view outside.

Straight ahead, Pallingham Church, Mum had written, and there it was, just where the road forked. *Methodist Chapel on right ... yes ... New Hall Lodge on left ... yes. The Grange (a big farm, on both sides)*; here it came – there it went – and then she saw the T-junction up ahead. The bus slowed down to wait at the major road, and Erica noticed a sign on the front of a house by the roadside; Calstead Post Office and Stores. There was nothing about Nudd, but perhaps Nudd was dead and only his name remained in people's minds. After all, there was no place called Mancroft any more, although there had once been, in Norman times. Erica had found this out on an old map at school. Up till then she had thought that Mancroft was St Peter's surname, and had often wondered about the other disciples: James and John Smith, Matthew Brown, Judas Iscariot Jones?

Taking a chance, she stood up and rang the bell once, according to the instructions round the bell-push, which was cream with a scarlet centre, like an uncooked jam tart. Erica pushed the jammy bit and the driver called: 'All right, all right, I've not forgotten you,' but not angrily, more as if he wanted her to feel wanted.

The bus stopped just round the corner in the main road, and the doors opened huffily with a loud breathy sigh, as if the effort had been too much for them. Erica stumbled out with the carrier bags, waved to the driver to thank him, and stood well back on the dusty verge, as the doors closed with an irascible snap and the bus drew away. She looked all round. Down on ground level again she could see where she was. Now she remembered the stores, with the untidy windows and the telephone kiosk outside, the electricity sub-station on the far side of the road near the willows, and, in the distance, a few hundred metres up the Happing road on the right, Hall Farm Cottage with its vegetable stall tacked on at the side and its garden full of fruit trees.

And there, coming down the road a little late to meet the bus, was Auntie Joan, waving. The bus, last link with Norwich, was out of sight and out of earshot. The holiday had begun.

Mum was thin. Auntie Joan went out where Mum went in, and further out where Mum went out, and she wore old clothes; not clothes that were old, but clothes that made *her* look old. She could have been Mum's mum rather than her sister, but although she was older, she was not that much older. Last time they had visited, Auntie Joan had complained that Mum worried too much about her figure and that dieting was unhealthy, look at all these young girls with anorexia. Mum said she wasn't a young girl, and anyway it was her duty to be thin because the rooms in the flat were so small. Air hostesses, Mum had said, had to be slim for the same reason, because wide air hostesses in narrow aircraft made the passengers feel overcrowded. 'Anyway,' Mum had said, 'look at Erica. Thinness run in our family, that just doesn't run on your side, Joan.' Perhaps this was why it had been the last visit. It must have been all of two years ago.

Auntie Joan came up to Erica and Erica looked her straight in the eye.

'Well, you've grown,' Auntie Joan said.

'Hello,' Erica said.

'How long've you been wearing glasses?'

'Since last Christmas,' Erica said. She thought it was not quite kind of Auntie Joan to mention her glasses, right off like that.

'They make you look like your brother,' Auntie Joan said.
'I thought your mum might've come with you. To see you were
safe, like.'

'She couldn't,' Erica said, as Auntie Joan turned herself
round and they set off up the road towards Hall Farm Cottage.
'She had to be at work at twelve, because they start serving
lunches at quarter past. She saw me onto the bus,' she added.
Mum worked on the lunch counter at the Dionysus Bodega in
Pottergate. It was supposed to be Greek and had vine leaves
all over the ceiling because it was a wine bar, but the people
who ran it were extremely English and came from Guildford.
Mum called them the Greek Family Robinson, because that
was the name of the gaffer, and said on the quiet that they were
a load of phonies, but she was happy enough to have the job,
especially with Dad worrying so much about the redundancies. It would not have done to have taken the day off, just to
make sure that Erica reached Calstead safely.

'I mean,' Auntie Joan was saying, 'the bus could've had an
accident. Or broke down. I shouldn't't've known where you
was.'

But you wouldn't have known where I was even if Mum *had*
been with me, Erica thought, but she had an idea that there
would be little use in pointing this out to Auntie Joan.

'You've grown so much you'll be taller'n Robert.' Auntie
Joan sounded peevish. Erica felt that it had been tactless of her
to grow taller than Robert, but on the whole she was glad.
Robert, as she recalled him, had been a big bore. As a little
bore he might be easier to put up with. They crossed the road,
passed the garden of Hall Farm Cottage and approached the
house from the rear, across an area of gravel.

The house stood sideways-on to the road, with the big
garden in front of it and at the far side, and the gravel patch
at the back where Uncle Peter parked his car. There was a
garage as well, but the car lived out of doors; there were too
many things in the garage to leave room for the car. Auntie
Joan opened the back door and they stepped down into the

narrow scullery, through that and into the kitchen. It was smaller than Erica remembered it, but she supposed that must be because she had grown so much, or so Auntie Joan seemed to think; and she, as it turned out, was not the only one who thought so. At the table, looking much busier with nails and wire than Erica would have expected, sat Robert. He raised his eyes from what appeared to be a scale model of the National Grid and said, 'Gar! What's that long thin thing you got there, Mum? That thing with four eyes, eh?'

He was even worse than she remembered; not even clever with his rudeness, simply rude. She wished that she could get Robert into a corner of the school playground with the Crowd, just for half an hour, until he learned what City wit could do, the great suety blob. If ever there was a real Norfolk dumpling it was Robert, and a bit underdone at that.

'Now, you get all that off of the table and let me lay the lunch,' Auntie Joan said. Robert began to remove his contraption, very slowly. Erica thought that he himself might have laid the table while Auntie Joan was out meeting the bus. At home she and Craig, and even Dad if he were on late turn, weighed in with the washing up and table laying when Mum was at work, because although Dad did not approve of men interfering with housework, as he cunningly termed it, he liked to eat on time. From what Erica recalled of life at Hall Farm Cottage, Robert and Uncle Peter would sooner go without food altogether than contribute anything towards the meal themselves.

'You take your things upstairs,' Auntie Joan said to Erica. 'That's the first room at the top, past ours.' Erica gathered her bags together and went up, relieved that Auntie Joan had sent her away instead of letting her stay in the kitchen, where she would have had to offer to help lay the table while Robert leaned on the dresser and watched.

The room was at the side of the house, not facing the road but looking out over the garden, across tree-tops and dykes, fields and more trees. The distant trees looked like the edge of

21

a wood, but Erica knew that in winter you could see daylight through them. Beyond the trees was the coast, where the sun would rise. The bed faced the window and Erica almost looked forward to next morning, when the rising sun would shine on her pillow and wake her up. At home, on the third floor at Tasburgh Court, her room faced north where neither sun nor moon shone in, although once she had looked out in the dark, during a power failure, and seen the Great Bear standing on its tail over Mousehold Heath.

She unpacked the carrier bags. This took about three minutes because she had had so little to bring; two changes of underclothes, a second pair of jeans, T-shirts and a sweater, her nightie and an arbitrary bundle of socks that might or might not contain a matching pair. Some, she felt sure, were Craig's. The second carrier contained hardware; brush and comb, sponge bag – which was a pedal-bin liner – a box of chocolates for Auntie Joan and the old-fashioned spectacles-case that Gran had given her because, Gran said, the soft, modern kind of case that the optician had provided might protect the lenses from being scratched, but would be no use if Erica sat on it. Gran was always sitting on her own glasses. They were held together in unlikely places by sellotape and elastoplast, solder and fuse wire. The case was hard and hinged and snapped shut like a beak.

Good cooking-smells drifted up the stairs and through the open door behind her. Erica heard Auntie Joan saying to Robert in the kitchen, 'Go you and call Erica down, there's a good boy.'

There was a long silence, and then Auntie Joan herself came to the foot of the stairs and called her to lunch. Robert was evidently afraid of straining his throat, but then Robert was afraid of straining anything; fingers, feet, *mind*, even, Erica thought derisively. That must be why he never thought; in case he sprained his brain; but if she called him Sprain-brain to his face he would never be able to work out why.

*

After lunch Erica and Auntie Joan cleared the table and washed up. Robert scarcely waited until they had moved the plates from in front of him before he was up and reassembling his infernal machine, all over his place mat.

'What is that you've got there?' Erica said, 'and give me that place mat – I want to wipe it.'

'You'll have to wait, then, won't you,' Robert said. He did not smirk with his face (because raw dough can't smirk, Erica told herself), but his voice was smirking. He knew that he could say what he liked, and Auntie Joan would not stop or reprimand him. Erica had to put down her dish towel and the bowl that she was drying, to stand out of the way while Auntie Joan went round with a broom, sweeping up after-lunch crumbs; but when she came to Robert's huge flat feet, she swept round them and did not even ask him to move. Still, she had probably learned by now that asking would have no effect.

Robert finally shifted himself to answer Erica's question.

'That's a rat trap,' he explained, running a fat finger up and down the wires. 'You hide that under the grass, see –'

'*Under* the grass? How? You dig a hole?'

'Nah, you put that in the grass, see, and the grass grow through that, and the old rats can't see that, see, and them old rats come along like this, see, and they get their nasty little feet caught up in these old wires, and then they starve to death, and we comes and picks them off and throw them away.'

'How will you make the rats run across it?' Erica said. 'I mean, you can't put up a notice, can you? *This way to the trap.*' She thought it was horribly cruel, but said nothing about that because it was only too clear that the trap would never work. Rats were, Erica considered, probably more intelligent than Robert. She polished the glass tumblers and imagined a small committee of rats meeting under the shed and planning a Robert trap, where Robert's nasty big feet would be caught. But it would take weeks to starve Robert to death. He could live off his surplus fat for ages.

'I'm going to make lots of them,' Robert announced,

smugly, 'and sell them at the fête next year. Old Miss Ames can have them on her stall with the corn dollies and lavender bags.'

'I shouldn't think anyone'd want your old rat traps on a gift stall,' Erica said. 'I mean, they aren't the kind of thing you can wrap up in nice paper and give people for presents. I mean, would you want to get a rat trap on your birthday? That'd be like getting a tin of slug pellets instead of sweets.'

'That's enough of that,' Auntie Joan said. She did not smile as she spoke, and Erica decided that she had better start learning the rules: Rule Number One, Robert need do no work; Rule Number Two, Robert could do no wrong; Rule Number Three, no one was allowed to be rude to Robert; and Rule Number Four, Robert himself could be as rude as he liked.

'Now then,' said Auntie Joan, wiping down the draining-board and even drying the base of the washing-up bowl, 'are you coming to help me in the garden, Erica?'

'Yes,' Erica said. She turned to Robert, once again absorbed by the rat trap. 'Are you coming, Robert?'

'I hent,' Robert said.

'Don't you want to help Auntie?'

'He don't have to if he don't want to,' Auntie Joan said, shrewishly, but Erica was unabashed. Rules after all were made to be broken, and she had managed to break most of them all at once.

Chapter Three

In the distance, from the direction of the coast road, she heard a motor cycle. The land was so flat, and sound carried so far, that the bike might have been miles away, but hearing it, as she stood there in the garden of Hall Farm Cottage, she was reminded suddenly, sharply, of all that she was missing back in Norwich. This time yesterday she had been sitting on the wall above the market, watching the motor cycles and staring at the great tower of St Peter Mancroft, with its pale stones and long green underwater windows.

Auntie Joan had gone indoors to prepare dinner before Uncle Peter came home from work, leaving Erica to collect and bring in the tools and trug. Erica thought of Mrs Pearson next door, who so badly wanted a garden, but if Mrs Pearson ever had a garden it would not resemble this one. Mrs Pearson dreamed of flowers and trailing creepers, little statues and urns with bulbs growing in them, and a big patch of stone paving where she could grow herbs. She had once described it all to Erica, as they sat drinking coffee in the Pearsons' kitchen, and she had shown her, in strictest secrecy, a plan that she had drawn; the lawns and beds and paths, each tiny flower coloured in with felt-tipped pens and every paving slab in place. *Real stone,* Mrs Pearson had said firmly, not concrete. They had spent all morning looking at it, and suggesting new plants to put in, but Erica had never mentioned it again, feeling that Mrs Pearson kept it so secret because she was afraid that she would never have a garden of her own. She bought her a hyacinth in a pot that flowered in time for Christmas, that year, but it hardly made up for not having a garden.

Auntie Joan's garden was nothing like the one that Mrs Pearson longed for. Last night, when Mum began to suspect that Erica was perhaps not quite so overjoyed by the prospect of a holiday in Calstead as she had hoped, she had said, 'You'll only be a mile from the sea ... and think of that huge garden!' Erica had known what the garden was like, all right, but she had forgotten how it flourished. She had not reckoned on everything being so green, and what was not green was blue. First the sky, bright blue, then the distant elms on the Tokesby road, next the soft heavy willows at Iken Fen, already a greener blue – the colour of mould on orange peel, Erica thought; the real bitter green of the sugar beet in the field across the dyke, then the garden itself, not one colour only but every shade from the bright budgerigar-green of spinach and lettuce to the gentle, almost grey bloom of the curtseying cabbage-leaves.

By the front door, not much larger than a bedspread, lay a rectangle of lawn, embroidered with dandelions and plantains, which Uncle Peter mowed with a scythe, when he remembered to. The rest of the garden, every square metre of it except for the too-narrow paths, was cultivated. As well as the beans and peas that grew alongside every path, there were beds of cabbages bordered with spinach, beds of lettuces bordered with radishes and spring onions, beds of Spanish onions and carrots in alternate rows, kohlrabi and calabrese, beetroot, turnips and swedes. Beyond the lawn lay the potato patch and the outdoor tomato plants, the gooseberry bushes and the raspberry canes.

26

A lot of it went into Auntie Joan's chest freezer that hummed and chirruped to itself in the garage, like a robot parrot; but the rest was sold, some at Calstead Stores, some from the little stall by the side entrance. All afternoon, while they had been gardening, people had walked up from the village or stopped their cars to buy vegetables. A square iron bell was tethered to the stall by a length of chain. If anyone wanted serving they could ring, and Auntie Joan would instantly drop whatever she was doing and hurry out to attend to them. Sometimes they heard a car draw up and could get there before anyone rang.

'Doesn't anyone ever pinch anything?' Erica had asked. She could imagine a bandit tourist cruising past very slowly, with the window wound down, and an arm whipping out to grab a cucumber or a bouquet of beetroot. 'People don't do that kind of thing *round here*,' Auntie Joan had snapped, implying that this was exactly the kind of thing that they did in Norwich. She thought that Norwich was a den of low life and illicit practices, where nothing was safe unless it was screwed to the floor. Robert never answered the bell, even when he was standing by the hedge watching someone ring it.

Erica piled the trowel and fork, secateurs, gloves and bast into the trug and stood up to carry it back to the house. As she rose she saw a little sheeny crescent of cobalt blue that blinked at her from among the beans. It was the eye in a peacock's tail-feather, the feather itself at least a metre long, the eye iridescent and perfect. She drew it out of the beans and held it up to the sun, where it glistered against the sky's lighter blue and glossed green and turquoise. Where had it come from? Auntie Joan certainly kept no peacock; the feather was just *there*, like an exotic flower that had grown from some mysteriously dropped seed. She looked up further, into the sky, wondering if a high-flying peacock had shed it while passing over, and for a moment, in her mind's eye, she saw the bird, tail spread like a flying fan, cruise across the sun, a feathery Concorde. Then she heard Uncle Peter's car grinding over the gravel behind the house, and hurried indoors.

By the time she had made a detour to put away the tools, Uncle Peter was in the kitchen. 'Well, hello stranger,' he said. He was not an effusive man. Erica held up the feather.

'Look what I found in the garden. Where did it come from – can I keep it?'

There was an appalling silence. Uncle Peter, and Robert, and Auntie Joan stood round the table and stared, as if she had held up a dripping dagger instead of a feather, and outside in the garden they heard a long and scornful squawk.

'That's where that came from,' Auntie Joan said, finally.

'Take that out of here,' Uncle Peter said. His eyes were small and murderous. 'Take that right out and lose it.'

Erica remembered that peacock feathers were supposed, by some people, to be unlucky, but she had not thought of Uncle Peter as being that sort of a person.

'They're not really unlucky,' she said. 'Mrs Pearson's got a whole bunch, in a jug. She's not had any bad luck ...' She hesitated. The Pearsons could not be described as positively lucky, either.

'Not unlucky,' Uncle Peter said. 'That's what that come off that's unlucky.'

'That bird,' Auntie Joan said, 'have ate everything. *Everything*. All them peas and beans I got through the drought, and lettuces ... carrot tops ... everything!'

'I never thought of them being called peacocks because they ate peas,' Erica said. 'Why aren't they called beancocks – or carrotcocks?'

This did not go down at all well.

'There's nothing funny in seeing your vegetables ate by other people's birds,' Auntie Joan said.

'Does that belong to someone?'

'Him up there,' Uncle Peter pointed through the scullery towards Happing. 'That architect bloke what keeps the daft animals.'

'What daft animals?'

'He've got pigs,' Uncle Peter said, 'but they hent ordinary

28

pigs; they're Vietnamese pot-bellied pigs. He've got ducks, but they hent ordinary ducks; they've got red beaks and he say they're Muscovy ducks. He've got a special kind of cat that have to be kept in water –'

'You're making that up,' Robert said.

'I hent,' said his father. 'I went round there once, to complain about the peacock – and there's all these white cats, swimming about in the pond. That's an ornamental pond, naturally. He've got two. One for the fish, which hent *ordinary* fish, naturally, and one for the cats. And his missus had got a pudding basin on the draining-board with this little kitten in it. And she says, "Little Mustapha is poorly. I'm just giving him a good soak." I says, "What'll you do then? Give him three hours on the bottom shelf at regulo 6?" She weren't amused,' said Uncle Peter.

Robert did not look much amused, either.

'I've heard of them,' Erica said. 'They're ever so rare. They come from Turkey, they're called Van cats.'

'I'd drown them,' Robert mumbled. 'I'd hold them under, them old cats.'

'And the peacock,' Auntie Joan said. 'That come down here every morning, and that gorge itself – on my vegetables.'

'There was two,' Uncle Peter said. 'He had another one, but that got out on the road one day and got a bit bent by a minibus. The driver was that upset. He gets out and knocks on the back door. "Excuse me," he says, "I think I've killed your peacock." "That hent mine," I says. "Come down the Bull and I'll buy you a drink." "But hent that valuable?" he says. I says, "You're telling me that's valuable. That's got thirty quid's worth of seedlings inside."'

'Us'll get that one day,' Robert said. 'Me and my traps or Dad and his gun.'

Erica was woken at five the next morning when Uncle Peter got up to shoot the peacock. This was nothing special, she learned later; he did it every morning. Lying in bed in the

29

room next door to the one where he slept with Auntie Joan, she could hear him tiptoe heavily about, making preparations. Out in the garden, unheard, the peacock too was making preparations. Erica propped herself on one elbow and looked out of the window, just in time to see the bird drop like a dozy paratrooper in evening dress from the roof of the shed in the next field where it had spent the night, the skirt of its tail spread expensively over the tarpaulin behind it. It disappeared for a moment behind the gooseberry bushes and then she saw its head emerge, like a periscope on the end of its long neck, proceeding in jerks along a row of dwarf beans.

In the next room the sash window went up as the peacock began industriously stripping the first of the day's beans from the plants. Erica heard the clack of a safety catch being removed. The peacock reached the end of the dwarf beans and recklessly showed its entire self for an instant before it swept its damp tail in a dewy arc through the grass; and simultaneously Uncle Peter let fly with both barrels.

Erica leaned her chin on the window-sill and watched the echoes rolling away through the green garden, the beans, the peas, the apple trees and the willows, over the dyke and the marshes to the woods and the Tokesby road. The peacock turned, looked vaguely in the direction of the house, and walked unhurriedly out of sight among the raspberry canes. Uncle Peter had sworn that the bird had more holes than eyes in its tail, but Erica could see that the nearest cabbage, an early Greyhound, was perforated like a colander.

Through the wall she heard Auntie Joan grumbling, 'Of course you didn't get that.' There was a prolonged bout of creaking as Uncle Peter broke the gun and settled back into bed where he began immediately to snore. Perhaps he had done the shooting in his sleep.

Erica knew that there was no chance that she would sleep again. Often at home she was woken early when Mr Pearson went to work. If the weather were fine he would wheel out his Honda into the road and up the street a little way before jumping on the kick-start, but if it were raining hard he would do it as he left the courtyard, right under Erica's window. On those mornings she never managed to fall asleep again, and would lie in bed reading old bike magazines, but there were no old bike magazines here. She had short-sightedly left them behind. Her ears were still rollicking from the percussion of the gun shot, and she guessed, from what Uncle Peter had said yesterday, that this was going to happen every morning, as it had been happening every morning for the past four months, ever since the day the peacock had first parachuted from the shed roof into the garden; and the peacock was no closer to meeting its maker than it had been on that fateful occasion when Uncle Peter and the peacock had met for the first time in the doorway of the greenhouse, Uncle Peter going in and the peacock coming out, with a smile from one side of its beak to the other according to Uncle Peter, leaving behind it a sad wreck of martyred seedlings.

She did not go downstairs until she heard Uncle Peter leaving for work, and the peacock could be seen ambling homeward, yodelling plaintively in the distance. 'Though what that have got to complain about,' Auntie Joan said, while being violent with bacon and eggs, 'I don't know. That've got a crop full of our beans this morning.'

'Perhaps that doesn't like having its tail shot off,' Erica suggested.

'If that don't like its tail shot off, that can stay on its own patch. I spent all summer watering them beans. You might go out after we've washed up. See what's left. Beth Nudd'll be along in a minute.'

Robert, knitting up rat traps in the corner, smiled, knowing that neither 'we' nor 'you' included him.

Chapter Four

Every day was the same. After a week Erica understood that nothing was going to change, ever, at Hall Farm Cottage. Each morning was exactly like the one before, each afternoon and each evening, except at the weekend, when Auntie Joan stopped polishing and Robert and Uncle Peter spent the afternoons and evenings in front of the television set. By the following Wednesday, Erica calculated, she had not seen a motor cycle more than once a day, and it was the same one each time, a feeble moped travelling between Happing and Polthorpe in the mornings, back again in the evenings.

Every morning Beth Nudd, from the shop at Calstead Corner, put a note through the door with a request for vegetables, but Auntie Joan's main retail outlet was the stall by the side gate. Each day, as soon as Beth Nudd's order had been made up, Auntie Joan would pack it all into her bicycle basket and take it down to the corner. While she was away, Erica arranged the remainder into tempting bundles and carted them out to the stall. When she came back Auntie Joan chalked on a blackboard a list of things that were for sale that day, peacock permitting.

32

The house was on the coast road from Cromer to Yarmouth, but as well as the people in cars who stopped to buy there were regular customers from the village. Erica could see why. At Nudd's Stores everything was piled into the window with what was there already, among pyramids of tins, hand cream, pegs, deodorants, flour and sugar and washing powder, beetroots and tomatoes lost among plastic buckets, runner beans in faggots propped against toilet rolls. On the stall it was all laid out invitingly, bundles of carrots with their greens still on, scrubbed and ready to gnaw, purple Desirée potatoes, cucumbers as long as rounders bats and tomatoes like cricket balls. But there was no suggestion, as at Nudd's, that you might actually get a cricket ball instead of a tomato, or find coat-hangers in with your stick beans.

Erica's first job, after breakfast, was to go out into the garden and gather the day's produce. Things happened at exactly the same time each day, so as she went down the path she always saw the Norwich bus turning the corner by Calstead Stores. It was a fearful temptation, because there was really nothing to stop her from sneaking down to Calstead Corner, or Iken Fen which was further along the road and out of sight, and catching the 705 back to the bus station, if only for a quick visit; but if she did that Auntie Joan would be hurt, and Mum would be worried if Auntie Joan were upset, and anyway, it would be breaking the rules of a holiday to nip off home in the middle of it, even for a couple of hours.

On Wednesday she watched the bus go by more forlornly than ever, for a letter from Mum had arrived yesterday after-noon. It had not said much – Mum was no hand at letter-writing – but it was, like the bus, a reminder of home. Like the bus, it had been in Norwich. The letter was on her bedside table and the bus was turning the corner without her.

Erica wished that she had her rubber boots to put on. Not only the grass was wet with dew; the plants dabbled at her legs with long moist fingers or pressed dribbly mouths against her hands. She was glad to put down the trug with its damp cargo and pause to open the greenhouse. Uncle Peter said that it was a cold house, meaning that it had no heating system, but even though the sun had not yet come round to that end of the garden, steaming through the wet leaves, it was already warmer in there than it was outside. Erica gathered the tomatoes, snug in her hand like fresh eggs, and wished that it really were eggs that she was collecting. If only Hall Farm Cottage really were a farm; searching for new-laid eggs in warm straw would have made a more promising start to the day than wading through the tidal surge of wet leaves, green, green, in search of more green things.

As she left the greenhouse she put up the peacock trap. This was a wooden frame, with chicken wire stretched across it, that slotted into the doorway. It was of Uncle Peter's making and was intended to keep the peacock out. If Robert had had anything to do with it, it would have been fitted with moving parts, hooks and rotating blades for dismembering the peacock. The original trap had been waist high but the peacock, apparently, had simply jumped over it. Erica was not sure whether or not to believe this. Such a hold did the peacock have over the minds and imaginations at Hall Farm Cottage that a kind of mythology was growing up round it. It was reputed to perform super-avian feats. It was prodigious. If Auntie Joan had claimed that it bestrode the lightning and nested in the sun Erica would not have been surprised.

Mist was rising off the sugar-beet field now. The way back to the house lay through the marrow patch, her least favourite part of the garden, although if she had been asked which was her favourite she would have been hard put to it to choose a place; possibly the gravel patch at the back where Uncle Peter left the car. Nothing grew there. She had no objections to marrows as such, although she did not enjoy eating them. They looked harmless enough at Harvest Festivals, when half the school turned up with marrows (and the other half with baked beans) and they were laid out in rows, like a bumper litter of enormous piglets, along the front of the platform. She

34

had always imagined that they grew in small staid clumps with smooth fat leaves, placid and porcine. Nothing had prepared her for the sight of the marrow bed at Hall Farm Cottage, overrun with wild rampaging vines, all barbed with spikes as vicious as those on rose or bramble – even the leaves were thorny – that escaped in all directions and climbed madly up hedge and tree, wherever they could gain a claw-hold. You could almost see them growing. They reared into the air like spiny snakes, wrapping tendrils resilient as rubber thongs round twigs, leaves, even blades of grass, and *hanging on*. Erica had a feeling that if she lingered too long to watch, one of those vines might silently reach her foot and begin to climb boldly, without stealth, up her leg, wrapping buttons and belt and fingers in those irresistible coils.

Already one was on its way up the Bramley. Among the green leaves and sober, small apples, only half ripe as yet, she could see the blaring yellow marrow-flowers, garish and un-expected, more like tropical blossoms in a jungle than English vegetables in a Norfolk garden. Down in the bed some juvenile marrows were already loitering with intent, not at all like piglets, unless they should be the farrow of a wild boar. She could see their pale rounded backs, swelling ... swelling ... nothing would stop them, and she hurried on, clasping the trug over her arm, before one of them could raise its bloated body from the damp earth and come after her, snorting and grunt-ing, nuzzling at her shoes with its snout. Back at home, three floors up at Tasburgh Court, she would have giggled at the thought of being chased up the garden by a wild tusked marrow, but not here. Here, even with the sun shining and a lark dancing somewhere above the branches of the Bramley, it was not so funny. Vegetables were rampant, vegetables ruled; and if they took a fancy to human flesh, who could stop them?

When she got back to the house the mail van was just driving away. It was eight o'clock. At home the post arrived at seven and the paper at eight; here the paper arrived at half past eleven, after the milk. At home the milk came before she was up, at ten past six. It was like living in Australia here, everything upside-down.

'Anything for me?' Erica asked, as she came into the kitchen and balanced the trug on the draining-board. She asked every morning, and again at three, when the afternoon delivery arrived, but there never was anything, except for yesterday's letter from Mum. There was no sign yet of Craig's postcard, but then she had not written to him either.

Auntie Joan shook her head and moved to the draining-board to begin sorting out the vegetables, but before she had laid hands on them a turnip rolled into the sink, under its own steam, and the whole pile shifted slyly. Erica was reminded of Mrs Pearson, who kept a coven of house-plants inside a great glass carboy in the corner of her living-room. Erica had gone round there one night to keep an eye on Barry Pearson while his mum nipped down to the doctor's, and while she was sitting there, all alone in the quiet room because Barry, then aged three months, was asleep and the telly had broken down, all the plants in the carboy had suddenly moved, silently, before settling back as if nothing had happened. Erica had shifted her chair after that, and had sat watching the carboy for three quarters of an hour until Mrs Pearson came home, half expecting a skinny hand to part the stalks and make room for some green unimaginable face to peer through, distorted by the thick flawed glass.

Mrs Pearson had explained, when she came back, that it was nothing unusual: after all, she said, the plants were growing all the time, weren't they? The leaves and stalks became tangled and bent together, Mrs Pearson said, and every now and again they untangled themselves; but Erica was not at all reassured, and went home as soon as she could. In a way it was worse to know that there was no one inside the carboy creeping about and disturbing the leaves. In her own room she had a mother-of-thousands plant that did not bear flowers, but grew small baby plants all round the edges of its own leaves, which

36

were fat and long like fleshy spearheads. When the baby plants dropped off, to set up home on their own, they grew hopeful little roots and lay about on the window-sill, waiting to be put into pots. After the incident with Mrs Pearson's carboy Erica gave the mother-of-thousands to Craig, who poured ink into the earth to see if the leaves would turn blue. It was an experiment he'd learned at school, he said, but the leaves turned yellow and the plant died, leaving thousands of orphans.

'Now,' said Auntie Joan, 'will you lay out the stall or take these –' she pointed to the vegetables left in the trug – 'down to Beth Nudd for me?'

Erica had not been entrusted with the Nudd delivery before, but she felt that the stall was her own special preserve, even though Robert was out there hunting toads with a bicycle spoke in the ditch alongside.

'I'll stay here,' she said. She liked handling the vegetables – once they were picked and harmless – liked arranging them in patterns, staking out the bell on its iron chain, waiting for customers. She was beginning to enjoy serving the customers, too. They were human beings, many of them in cars that came from places other than Calstead, where there were street-lights and fire hydrants, traffic lights and pelican crossings, petrol fumes, car parks, parking meters, 'stop' signs and 'go' signs. She knew that she must never ask for, or accept, lifts in strange cars, but on the stillest, greenest days, when nothing moved but the leaves and there was no sound but the peacock squawking near by and far away, the smallest, dingiest car looked like a magic chariot that would carry her home if only she had the nerve to step in and leave the stall standing unattended by the roadside. She never did. She never would.

Auntie Joan wheeled her bicycle round to the back door and began packing Mrs Nudd's order into the freezer basket that was strapped to the handlebars. When that was done she walked it, as if it were a capricious and undependable pony, across the gravel and into the road, before mounting and riding unsteadily away, with the carrot tops nodding over her basket like hair on a severed head, while Erica stood by the stall with an armful of leeks and watched her, hearing the bicycle creaking rheumatically down the road into the quiet morning distance.

She was just building a teepee of leeks round a cabbage, like lady fingers adorning the sides of a rich jelly, when she heard the creaks coming back again. Auntie Joan applied the brakes before she began to get off, and got off before she turned the corner onto the gravel.

'I forgot,' she said.

Erica waited. Auntie Joan was not chatty. Her remarks came in short rows of words, like lists, and you sometimes had to wait a long while for another item to be added to the list. Auntie Joan climbed out of the bicycle and leaned it against the wall. 'I've got to go into Polthorpe,' she said. 'I've got to see Elsie Wainwright.'

Erica lined up the cucumbers.

'Only I can't.'

Erica pointed towards Calstead Corner and the telephone kiosk.

'Can't we ring?'

'There's something to bring back. Something your Uncle wanted. Elsie'll know what that is.' Erica waited again. 'And there's the shopping. I forgot that, too.'

Erica cottoned on. 'You want me to go?'

'That'd be a help,' Auntie Joan said. 'I don't mind going, that hent that, but I've to clean the village hall this morning. That's my turn. There's a meeting tonight. And the ironing's still to do. If you go into Polthorpe for me, you could drop that off, on the way.' She pointed to the contents of the freezer basket.

'You mean, take the bike?' Erica said.

'I didn't mean you to walk,' Auntie Joan said. Erica had been thinking of the bus, but she did not fancy walking down to Calstead Corner with that lot in a string bag.

'You can do the shopping while you're at it,' Auntie Joan was saying, as Erica eyed the bicycle. 'Come on in. I'll give you a list. And the message for Elsie.'

Auntie Joan sat down at the table to compose her shopping list. Erica picked up the message. It was in an old envelope, several times used. On the front it said, in typewritten letters, *To Mr C. J. Hemp*. Someone, presumably C. J. Hemp himself, had crossed out *C. J. Hemp* and written *P. D. Myhill*, which was Uncle Peter, underneath in blue biro. Uncle Peter had crossed out *P. D. Myhill* and scribbled, also underneath, in pencil, *Wainwright*. Erica took a pencil from the dresser and added an *s* to the original *Mr* so that the address now read *To Mrs Wainwright*, here and there. It occurred to her that Elsie might be a miss, but most of Auntie Joan's friends seemed to be married and it was very likely that she would not read the address anyway, what there was of it.

'Where does Elsie Wainwright live?' Erica said.

'I don't know,' Auntie Joan said. 'Just go to Mercury Motor Cycles and give them the letter. There'll be someone there that know about that, if Elsie aren't.'

'*Motor cycles?*' Erica said.

'That's right.' Erica did not pursue the subject any further. Auntie Joan would not be interested in any case, but the sooner Erica left for Polthorpe, the sooner she would be there herself, at Mercury Motor Cycles, seeing what there was to be seen.

She set off feeling insecure and foolish in the saddle. She would not have chosen to ride Auntie Joan's bicycle any distance in public, and she would not have allowed herself to be seen even standing near it in Norwich. Had she not come to Calstead by bus she would have brought her own bicycle with her, crossbar, drop handlebars, twenty-six-inch wheels and all. Auntie Joan's machine looked as if it had been hand-forged by a blacksmith out of hot iron back in the sixteenth century. It wore what appeared to be a fillet of umbrella round the rear mudguard to protect Auntie Joan's skirt at beet-lifting time, the wheels were unaligned, and one handlebar seemed higher than the other. Erica thought that it must be similar to riding an old deformed cow, and now that she was aboard the beast the creaking sounded less like ancient joints than the pitiful moans of some creature that was dying from a loathsome disease of the lungs.

But it was a bicycle; it was a machine; someone had *made* it. It had spokes and brakes and pedals, not leaves and stems and roots; it leaked oil, not sap; it was black, not green; and it was carrying her back towards civilization.

Chapter Five

Just seeing the telephone kiosk outside Calstead Stores made Erica feel closer to real life. She carried the vegetables into the shop, while Mrs Nudd held the door open, and hung about pointedly while Mrs Nudd arranged them in the window, waiting for her to pay. She needed the money to buy Auntie Joan's shopping in Polthorpe, but hardly liked to say so in case Mrs Nudd thought that Auntie Joan should be doing her shopping at Calstead Stores.

'Enjoying your holiday, then?' Mrs Nudd asked, shifting a box of washing powder and a camping stove to make way for some cucumbers. Erica noticed that a very old cucumber, probably one of last week's, had curled up and died, unnoticed, behind an economy-sized bag of dog biscuits. It had gone soft and furry, shrunk to only half of its original size.

'I said, enjoying your holiday, then?' Mrs Nudd repeated. Seeing where Erica's glance lay, she picked up the deceased cucumber between thumb and forefinger and tossed it out of the doorway.

'Oh *yes*,' Erica said. 'Ever so. Thanks.'

41

'I expect you're glad to get away from all that noise and traffic for a bit. I don't know how your mum stand that.'

'She's used to it,' Erica said, always surprised to be reminded that Mum had grown up in Pallingham, the next village. Auntie Joan could never understand how Mum could bear to go and live so far away. Auntie Joan seemed to think that just moving the mile and a half from Pallingham to Calstead had been a voyage to foreign territory. Uncle Peter was really foreign. He came from Happing, five miles away.

'She want to come out here for a bit; get a bit of peace and quiet,' Mrs Nudd said.

'She's getting a bit of peace and quiet while I'm away,' said Erica, 'and my brother's gone camping in Yorkshire.'

'All that traffic!' said Mrs Nudd.

'We live on the third floor. That's flats,' Erica said, and thought longingly of Tasburgh Court where the bikers roared up and down the hillside across the street and the sodium lamp on its tall post shone in with a hellish orange glare if she left the bedroom curtains open.

'And the muggers!'

'We've never been mugged,' said Erica.

'And the *rates*. I couldn't stand that,' Mrs Nudd mourned, just as if someone had threatened to make her stand it.

You don't have to, Erica thought. I have to stand being here instead.

She collected the money and went out, intending to cycle over the ejected cucumber and cut it in two, but in the meantime a car had gone by and squashed it flat. She wheeled the bicycle round it, very carefully, not quite liking to look, as if it had been a run-over hedgehog or frog.

It would be two miles to Polthorpe if she cut up past the Methodist Chapel, and three miles if she went through Pallingham. Erica was in a hurry to get among people and traffic, but the Methodist route ran across country, while the other road passed two farms, Pallingham Post Office and the huge service station that hired out agricultural machines. It went past council houses, too; there might be children. There were no children in Calstead except for infant twins further up the Happing road and Robert, who in Erica's opinion scarcely counted as a child at all; no wonder the school had been closed. Someone was living in it now, and the playground, with its painted netball court and hopscotch squares, had become the parking space for three cars. Erica thought that children who needed their hopscotch laid on by the council deserved to die out.

There was no sign of life by the council houses either, except for a boy who leered at her over a fence and shouted, 'Why don't you get off and milk it?' Erica looked round to make a rude gesture, and fell off instead. At home, by Tasburgh Court, the boy would have come out jeering, spoiling for a fight, and there would have been one, but here, when Erica picked herself up and looked over the fence in her turn, she found that he had already forgotten about her and was peacefully hoeing an onion bed at the side of his house.

'Furt'loizer!' Erica yelled, across his tidy garden. It was what she had heard Manchester United fans shouting out of train windows at Norfolk stations, in the hope of demoralizing Canaries' supporters. The boy took no notice. Perhaps he had never been close enough to a train to understand the insult. He'd probably never *heard* of Manchester United, or even of Manchester. Probably, Erica muttered to herself, he'd never heard of the Canaries, either. Probably never even been to Norwich, *probably* didn't even know it existed ...

Erica herself was none too sure where Manchester lay, but at least she did know that it existed. It must do. It was where United came from. She climbed back onto the bicycle and rode on.

Halfway up Polthorpe Street – I suppose they mean High Street, Erica thought – was a big building with Town Hall carved on a stone tablet outside. Erica had imagined Polthorpe to be a village, but it was doing its best to look like a town. Pedalling up the Street she counted four supermarkets, two banks, two butchers, three greengrocers – *more* vegetables

43

– and an ironmongery. Her nose told her that the area boasted at least one chippy, and there was even a little betting shop lurking furtively down a loke, but she could not see Mercury Motor Cycles. There was a garage, Marsh's Service Station, with petrol pumps and several cars outside, but no bikes; push bikes or motor bikes. She rode up as far as the old railway station and found that she had passed right through Polthorpe. There was nothing in front of her but the main road, stretching away on either hand to Norwich and Yarmouth, beyond it the sewage works and, to one side, the Broad. Above the willows on the far side of the road she could see the gliding tips of white triangular sails, like an encampment of bell tents, mysteriously on the move. The staithe and the boat station were over there too, but she had visited them before. Everything there was meant for floating; no wheels.

Erica turned the bicycle in a huge unwieldy circle and coasted back again, with one regretful look over her shoulder at the road sign behind her: NORWICH 18 MILES. It was no distance; it was half the world away.

This time she noticed a pet shop, a house with a dentist's brass plate outside, Polthorpe Radio Services and a shop window full of clothes for middle-aged ladies to go to parties and weddings in; not the kind of thing that Mum or Auntie Joan would be seen dead in, although for very different reasons; but before long she found herself back at the lower end of Polthorpe Street, outside the Co-op, and this time she was sure that she had not passed Mercury Motor Cycles. She parked Auntie Joan's bicycle against a street-lamp standard and went into the Co-op to do the shopping. When she reached the check-out she paid for the groceries and asked, 'D'you know where Mercury Motor Cycles is?'

It was a good thing that the assistant had an automatic cash-register. All the time she was adding up the cost of Erica's purchases she was talking to a friend on the next counter, and could hardly bear to stop for long enough to glance at Erica and mutter, 'On th'industrial estate.'

44

'Industrial estate?' Erica said. Where on earth could that be? There were industrial estates round Norwich, on the Outer Ring Road. Polthorpe would have fitted comfortably into any of them, several times over. 'Where's that?'

The check-out girl pointed vaguely towards a stack of paper towels. The industrial estate, it seemed, was in the stock room, behind the door that said *Private, Staff Only*.

'How do I get to that?'

'That's back of Marsh's,' the girl said. 'Up the Street. Turn right.'

Erica went out and tried to get her bearings. Marsh's, she remembered, was the service station. It figured that a service station would be on an industrial estate. More cheerfully she began to wheel the bicycle back up the Street, drawn on by visions of factories, floodlights, great double gates and chain-link fences on concrete posts like giant tyre-levers, with notices that said THIS AREA IS PATROLLED BY GUARD DOGS and CAUTION – HEAVY PLANT MOVING; but that reminded her of the marrows and she changed the subject.

She was held up outside the service station by an articulated lorry that had tried to alter direction, in the middle of Polthorpe's narrow thoroughfare, by reversing onto the forecourt. It was now jammed like an arm that had gone into a tight sleeve elbow first, and a line of cars was forming on either side of it, patiently, not like cars in Norwich that would have been hooting and belching angry exhaust. Perhaps they realized that here it would make no difference how angry they became. Several people had stopped to watch and shop assistants were standing in doorways, interestedly discussing the artic's chances of getting itself out again this side of Christmas.

Erica waited until the driver cut the engine and there was no chance that the lorry would burst murderously out of its strait-jacket as she went by, then scuttled across the forecourt while Auntie Joan's bicycle bucked and skidded beside her, trying to go its own way like a supermarket trolley with locked wheels.

Now she saw that on the white front wall of the service station were a number of painted signboards one above the other, with arrows that pointed towards the mouth of an alley, at the side of the garage, paved with mud and old half-bricks. There were half a dozen of them, beginning at the bottom with *Polthorpe Joinery: Pallets, Fences, Broadland Fibreglass, Mike Hudson, welding, all types* and another, all in lower-case hand-lettering, *william birdcycles*. Erica got no further than William Birdcycles. Was his name William Bird, purveyor of bicycles, or was he Mr Birdcycles? Or did he in fact sell birdcycles, and if so, what were they? Then she noticed that on the far side of the alleyway was a standing shut/open sign that said, quite clearly, *Mercury Motor Cycles*. She wondered how she had missed it before, because on the disc part, which swung round and round when the wind blew, was an air-brushed design of a man in a winged helmet and sandals with wings on the heels, wearing a short Greek tunic like someone on an educational poster at school and riding a motor cycle. On the flip side of the disc it said simply *Agents for Honda*, but the man was not riding a Honda. His machine was a beautiful BSA Gold Flash, picked out very accurately in real gold paint. Erica took her own bicycle firmly by the handlebars, wrenched its head round to the right and started down the alley. On the wall was another sign, a sneaky, hand-painted one that looked as if it did not want to be noticed: *J. R. Bowen, Plumber*. Erica came out at the far end of the alley.

She was in a long yard, surrounded by low concrete buildings roofed with corrugated iron. One or two had open doors and there were three vehicles standing about; a van, a derelict-looking Ford and a total wreck; but she could see no chain-link fencing, no guard dogs, no floodlights, and there was no trace of heavy plant, moving or otherwise. The only plants in view were a thicket of fireweed and a meagre buddleia bush. In the fireweed a small male child with a large head that made him look remarkably like a tadpole was poking about with a stick, and, to complete the picture of decrepit domesticity, an elderly black and white cat, with a muzzle so shrunken by age that she seemed to have false teeth, sat washing her paws in the sunshine. Erica stood appalled. It might just as well have been a muddy farmyard. At any moment one of the double doors might open and a herd of cows or a pig come out. Then she heard the reassuringly urban sound of a compressor. Looking round she saw a row of motor cycles lined up outside one of the few premises that were already open, and in the gloom beyond the bikes, inside the doorway that yawned darkly like a cave, the sparks and burning beam of a welder at work. The compressor stood throbbing near-by, looking like an armoured wheelbarrow for use by entrenched gardeners who had to weed under fire. Once more Erica parked Auntie Joan's bicycle, which should be feeling more than ever like a cow in these surroundings, in the fireweed, took the envelope out of the freezer basket and went inside.

The welder looked up, saw her and laid his torch aside. He seemed to have finished whatever he was doing, for he removed his mask and came towards her, pulling off heavy gauntlet gloves.

'What can I do you for?' he said.

Erica said, 'I'm looking for Elsie Wainwright. I've got a letter here from my Uncle Peter – Peter Myhill, out at Calstead.'

'Where else?' said the welder. He was a young man in a blue boiler suit, but it was hard to see his face. His hair looked exactly like the camouflage on a flak helmet intended to disguise soldiers as plants. The oil on his face added to the illusion of a commando blacked up for a night raid. He ran his hands through his hair, making Erica wonder if he were wiping off grease in it, and said, 'Let's have it here, then.'

'Will you give it to Elsie Wainwright?' Erica said.

He said, 'I'm Elsie Wainwright.'

Erica looked at him, up and down, looked at the name on the envelope, and back to him again. It was clear that, after all, Elsie Wainwright was neither Mrs nor Miss.

Chapter Six

Elsie held out his hand. Erica gave him the letter. 'I reckon he'll be wanting his jump leads,' said Elsie.

'Who will?'

'Your Uncle Peter,' Elsie said. 'This is by way of being a gentle reminder.'

'You don't need a gentle reminder,' said a voice from behind the compressor. 'The only thing that'd jog your memory is a brisk blow to the back of the neck with a blunt instrument.'

Out of the darkness loomed a strange person. It was a very fat man, only about as old as Elsie but half as big again, wearing jeans and a black T-shirt with a human skeleton printed on it in bone white; ribs, spine and pelvis, with collar bones, which would have looked startling on a thin wearer and in a way looked even more startling on him. The ribs were all bunched together on a level with his armpits, and the pelvis, which should have covered his hips, was stretched across his stomach so that the skeleton looked like the disarrayed bones of a caveman, buried under something heavy and dug up again by archaeologists.

The fat skeleton saw Erica staring, but like most people

48

could not tell what she was staring at because of her glasses. He said, 'If you wore them over your eyes instead of on the end of your beak, you wouldn't have to squint.'

'Out of your coma then, Bunny?' Elsie said, pleasantly. 'The Duchess brought her Puch in this morning. It failed the MOT. Take a look, will you?'

'Why can't she join the queue like everyone else?' Bunny grumbled. Erica adjusted her glasses and continued to stare. There was nothing remotely rabbity about him. His front teeth did not stick out, his ears were small, especially compared to the rest of him. Possibly he had a secret passion for lettuce.

'Because she's the Duchess,' Elsie said. 'If she joined queues she wouldn't be the Duchess, would she?'

'You shouldn't encourage her,' Bunny said, morosely. 'Encouraging people like that just prolongs the oppression of the working classes.'

'What would you know about the working classes?' Elsie said. 'The old girl's chairs aren't at home. Better to let her do a little queue-jumping than risk high strikes out there in the yard.'

'We could charge people to come and watch,' Bunny said, and lumbered out into the sunlight, where he bent over a motor cycle near the end of the line outside the double doors. He was not wearing bones on his back.

'Is she really a duchess,' Erica asked, 'this lady?'

'She thinks she is,' Elsie said, 'and she's near as dammit got everybody else convinced. Now ... jump leads ...'

There was a long counter down one side of the shop. Elsie went behind it and bent out of sight, foraging. Erica, gradually recovering from shock, stood looking round. She was not quite sure why she should feel so surprised; perhaps because nothing could be more different from Hall Farm Cottage and she had not been expecting it. The shop was dark and gloriously greasy. Its concrete floor was a great grey map stained with islands and continents of spilled oil. The ceiling was low, with things hanging from it like in the delicatessen on Timber Hill

49

at home, only these things were not foreign sausages but fragments of motor cycles; mudguards and wheels, tyres and fuel tanks with wonderful designs air-brushed onto their flanks. One was sketched with ferny curlicues, one had a staring green eye painted on either side and a third was coated in gold fish-scales. All along one wall stood steel shelving units stacked with spanners and pliers, wrenches, gauges, rods, drifts and spoke threaders, oil cans and boxes of spares; and in one corner was a little glass-walled booth with a high stool in it and a shelf bearing piles of papers, invoices impaled on spikes and an oily white telephone. Erica thought that if she owned a repair shop she too would have a white telephone. It looked businesslike.

In the middle of the floor, balanced on oil cans, stood another skeleton, the frame of a motor cycle, stripped down and wheelless. Erica went over and examined it carefully, an inspection that told her that it had recently been lacquered over its dark red paint and was hardening off. On a bench near-by lay its front forks and tank. The forks were red, too, and there were no ferns or fish scales on this tank. Erica knew that it would be sacrilege to do anything to this particular bike except restore it as faithfully, lovingly and respectfully as skill allowed. She wondered which model it might be, and would have asked Elsie, only there was no sign of him and no sound from behind the counter. He seemed to have vanished, and she feared he had tiptoed out while she was examining the restoration work. Perhaps the counter could conceal the mouth of a burrow (where Bunny lived?) into which Elsie had tunnelled. She looked over the top and saw his back. He was on hands and knees and really did seem to be burrowing, for first one hand, then the other, reached out behind him and deposited something on the floor. A stack of boxes and dirty paper bags was growing round him and he seemed quite happy, like a hamster rearranging its bedding. Erica left him to it and went back to the open double doors to look out over the yard, where Auntie Joan's bicycle was browsing among the fireweed. It was now half-past nine, and the yard was waking up.

Along either side more doors were opening, and artefacts were appearing outside various premises: a stack of pallets by one, a couple of glassfibre hulls and a canoe outside another; although there was nothing that could possibly be a birdcycle. Two vans drove in from the far end of the yard, and here and there was the tadpole child, darting and skittering. Along the alley from the street came a frog on a Honda, his four-stroke nattering back at him from the high walls on either side. He circled the yard, bouncing loosely over ruts and broken bricks, before turning back to halt in front of Erica. He removed the crash helmet that concealed his entire head and said, 'Elsie about?'

Erica gaped at him. He was wearing a green boiler-suit and his helmet was green with a wide yellow stripe fore and aft. Without it he appeared quite normal, a bit spotty perhaps, but definitely a human being. In it he had looked so like a frog, with his knees up and his head drawn into his shoulders, that Erica almost expected him to inflate below the chin and croak.

'Elsie about?'

'In there.' She jerked her thumb over her shoulder.

The frog climbed off his machine and wheeled it into the shop.

'Else!'

Elsie's voice from under the counter said, 'That you, Kermit?'

'That is.'

'D'you want a word?'

'Brought the bike along.'

'Wheel her in.'

'Did.'

'Good.'

Erica lolled in the doorway, gazing. Was the frog called Kermit because he looked like a frog, or had he grown to look like a frog because he was called Kermit? He hung his green frog's head over his arm by the chin strap and waddled out, bowlegged, nodding to Erica as he went. His flat-footed boots

51

slapped the muddy ground like flippers. Over by the vans a little voice began to yelp, 'Dad! Dad!' and the child who looked like a tadpole cantered towards him.

'What you doing here, then?' Kermit said. 'Where's your mum?'

'She's over Uncle Alan's, cleaning out.' The tadpole hopped about, arms waving. His mum and Uncle Alan could be anywhere, including on the roof.

'Well, you stick close with her and don't go breaking nothing. And stay you out of Elsie's,' Kermit admonished it.

Elsie's own urgent hissing called her attention indoors.

'Is that the Gremlin?'

'The what?'

'A little lad – big head.'

'That's right.'

'Keep him out of here. Head him off.'

'I don't think he's coming over here anyway. Why d'you call him the Gremlin?'

'Because when he gets into things they go wrong.'

Erica watched the frog part company with his tadpole as they took off in opposite directions, and went back into the shop.

'I thought it looked more like a tadpole,' Erica said.

Elsie straightened up from behind the counter. 'I suppose it would, being Kermit's,' he said. 'Karen – his mum – Mrs Kermit, her brother-in-law runs the fish shop. His old lady's supposed to do the cleaning but she put her back out and Karen helps him. I always know when Mrs Catchpole's back's playing up if the Gremlin's about.'

Erica wondered if Kermit's Karen's brother-in-law's old lady was his wife, his mum, or just an old lady employed by him.

'. . . and the Gremlin,' Elsie was saying, 'likes coming in here to pass the time. He can't take a hint, that lad. Why don't you go over to Yerbut's and ask him to wire you up? Why don't you drop into Rat's Castle and get Jack to nail

52

you to the wall? Why don't you go back to your Uncle Alan and get deep-fried? But he just hangs around here, prodding. He's got a special long stick, specially for prodding things. "What's this here?" he says. *Prod.* "What's that for?" *Prod.* "What does this do?" *Prod. Clang, splat, kaput!* "It doesn't do anything, *now*," I tell him.'

'Yerbut?' Erica said. She saw from the direction of Elsie's pointing finger that Yerbut's place must be the back premises of Polthorpe Radio Services in the Street.

'He argues,' Elsie said. 'Everything you say to him, he goes, "Yer, but..." What else could we call him?'

'But what's his name?'

'Corbet.'

Yerbut Corbet? The Gremlin went by, his prodding stick at the ready. 'Why doesn't his mum look after him?' Erica said.

'Yerbut's mum? He hasn't got one. They put him together on a bench, out of spares.'

'No, the Gremlin's mum.'

'Look after him? What with, a sub-machine-gun? She does look after him, according to her lights. She calls it reasoning. "You have to *reason* with them," she says. She's read too many books. "Now then, pet, we don't do that, do we?" *Prod!* She'd be all right with a knot in her neck,' Elsie said, reflectively.

Conversation with Elsie was like flicking quickly through a book of pictures that had nothing to do with the words printed underneath. Already the yard was coming to life with strange people; strange people with strange names. Even the buildings were beginning to sound bizarre – Rat's Castle? Erica said quickly, 'Did you find the leads?'

'Leads?'

'Uncle Peter's jump leads, that I came for.'

There was a long pause.

'Not as such,' Elsie said, finally. 'They'll be about somewhere. I'll get somebody to bring them round.'

'I could come in for them another time,' Erica suggested, having suddenly realized that there was no longer anything to keep her there, and that unless she thought of a good excuse, there would be nothing to bring her back again. In a few minutes she would be riding away into the green desert of Calstead, never to return.

'You do that,' Elsie said, 'if it's no trouble. You didn't come specially, did you?'

'No, I was shopping. I'm staying in Calstead for the holidays.'

'I thought I hadn't seen you around,' Elsie said. 'And are you enjoying it?' Unlike most people who asked her that, he sounded uncertain.

'Oh yes; ever so,' Erica said. She looked round at the fireweed where the wrought-iron cow was ruminating drunkenly; a cow with a crumpled horn. She moved reluctantly towards it.

'Mind the San Andreas Fault,' Elsie called after her.

'You what?'

'That crack in the kerb on the way out. The Duchess came in the other day and jammed the front tyre of her Puch in it. Took a long time to lever her out. I told the council but they said it was up to Howlett's.'

'Who's Howlett's?'

'The landlord. Howlett's Industrial Estate.'

Erica looked all round her again. Behind her was Elsie's cavernous shop, in front, the little garages and stables, open windows in back premises, the mud, the fireweed and, somewhere, Rat's Castle. In the distance the Gremlin ran about, prodding and yoiking, Bunny crouched near-by alongside the Duchess's Puch that had jammed in the San Andreas Fault, and a smell of fish hung damply over all.

'Where is that?'

'Where's what?'

'The industrial estate.'

'This is it,' Elsie said.

'But that's only a yard.'

'I reckon you come from the big city, lady,' Elsie drawled. Erica knew sarcasm when she heard it, and flushed.

54

'I thought there'd be factories.'

'Well, Jack makes pallets – you could call him a factory. And there's the fibreglass boys, and Bill Birdcycle, only he's closed all day Wednesday. He's up at the other end, renovating a wreck. He thinks he might hire it out to television companies who need authentic historic background material.' Elsie was indicating the distant heap of junk that Erica had seen on the way in.

'Is his name really Birdcycle?'

'No, but he does lousy lettering,' Elsie said, obscurely.

'Can I get out at that end?'

'Follow the track and you'll come into Broad Street. Watch out for Copernicus. See you . . .'

Erica mounted one pedal of the cow with the crumpled horn and scooted over the mud and bricks, past the open doors, the Gremlin, Bill Birdcycle and his scrap heap. In the middle of the track was a craterous pothole with yellow water at the bottom. Erica wobbled round it and reached the corner of Broad Street. Now she mounted the iron cow and rode back along the side road, turning left into the Street. This time she kept her eyes open and saw the mouth of the alleyway before she passed it, with its swinging sign, the great crack in the kerb that must be the San Andreas Fault, and the glimpse of the strange land beyond; the industrial estate.

So far the journey had been uneventful. The articulated lorry had freed itself after all, she had not got jammed, like the Duchess, in the Fault, and she had managed to avoid Copernicus, whoever he might be.

Chapter Seven

Erica decided that she would write a letter to Mum and Dad after tea, when the table was cleared, but there might be a long while to wait. Tea was never begun until Uncle Peter came in from work, and he was often late. This evening it looked for a while as if he would be early, but just as he was putting the car away Ted Hales, who lived across the road and kept pigs, called to him for a quick word, and now Uncle Peter had been there for a good twenty minutes, he on one side of the thorn hedge, Ted on the other, gossiping in the way that housewives are supposed to do over their back fences. It was the same at home. Mum and Mrs Pearson might occasionally snatch a word across the concrete barrier that separated their balconies, but it was Dad and Mick Pearson who stood conversing for hours together about pigeons or snooker, or both, Dad with his hands in his pockets and Mick with a pigeon on his head so that he looked like a statue in a park. Uncle Peter was always suggesting that Auntie Joan spent half her time, when he was not watching, talking to friends. He called it mardling, but Erica had never seen Auntie Joan mardling with anyone, she was too busy; while Ted seemed to hide behind his hedge especially to buttonhole anyone who was passing, mardling away like nobody's business. Even people who stopped to buy vegetables at the stall got caught by Ted.

Ted's pigs lived indoors in a row of sheds and could be heard from the garden, roaring and snorting, sometimes shrieking so loudly that at first Erica had imagined that the sheds must house savage bulls. Now she assumed that they housed savage pigs, only barely contained by the frail wooden walls.

Uncle Peter came in at last and spent a long time washing at the kitchen sink.

'Any sign of my jump leads?' he asked, over his shoulder.

Auntie Joan looked at Erica. 'There hent. Erica went along. I don't know what the excuse was this time.'

Uncle Peter turned very slowly and looked over his other shoulder at Erica.

'You went to the shop?'

'I went to Mercury Motor Cycles,' Erica said, 'on Howlett's Estate. El – Els – Mr Wainwright couldn't find the leads. I said I'd go back again.'

'I've been going back for them jump leads for three months now,' Uncle Peter said. He spoke so heavily that it was impossible to tell when he was amused, or sad, or bored or, as now, when he was annoyed. He was never excited; his tick-over was too slow. Possibly this was why he had spent so long talking to Ted. Anyone else would have said what he had said in five minutes, but it had taken him twenty. Erica was always surprised that he could get angry enough to go after the peacock with a gun, while it was Robert who sat at the table devising traps for it. He sat there now, casting wistful glances at the dresser where his prototype caterpillar snare lay in an indecipherable tangle of hairpins and corks. The rat trap languished in the garage, abandoned. No one who had not been told in advance would have taken it for a caterpillar snare, although Robert had planned it meticulously and had blueprints.

57

'Well, shall I?'

'Do what?'

'Go back again?'

'Best you do.' Uncle Peter dried his hands. 'Best we keep going in relays until he do find them. He've been promising me them leads since May.'

'Perhaps we should all go together,' Erica said, 'so that he'd notice.'

'He'd not notice if we went in with a tank.' Erica recalled a similar remark of Bunny's. 'He've got that much on his mind that take him a week to see what's under his nose. I don't know why someone so slow-thinking as Elsie took to motor bikes in the first place, them being so fast.'

Erica thought that it was a cheek for someone as slow-speaking as Uncle Peter to talk about Elsie being slow. Auntie Joan said, 'Elsie hent slow, he's just always thinking about something else. Never what you want him to think about.'

'You want him to think about something,' Robert said, shoving his oar in, 'you got to give him a week's notice. Time you get back, he've started to think about that.' He grinned, as if he had come up with something clever. Erica withered him privately.

'He've been thinking about my jump leads for three months,' Uncle Peter said. He was moving towards the table. At any moment, tea *might* begin. It would not be a good idea to sidetrack anyone now, in case the meal were delayed even further while they thrashed the matter out, still standing up and frozen in their positions. Erica thought she knew what the trouble was. No one at Hall Farm Cottage seemed able to move and think at the same time. It was strange how much more hungry, really pitifully hungry, you could feel when you were ready to eat and couldn't – far worse than if you just wanted food and knew that you would get it – but without thinking of the consequences Erica said, 'Why's he called Elsie?'

As she might have known they would, everybody stopped

58

moving. Auntie Joan said, 'His mother called him Lynden, but she didn't like that when she'd said that a few times, I reckon. So she called him Elsie. He've always been Elsie.' After a moment, she added, 'So they say. He hent local.'

They removed to the living-room after tea, where Auntie Joan and Uncle Peter settled in front of the television set. Erica shared the table with Robert, who rolled back the red chenille cloth and set up his caterpillar trap. It was constructed along the lines of a lobster-pot, on the principle that once the victim was lured in it could not find its way out again past the spines of the hairpins. Erica imagined that it would be a tedious business visiting the individual traps every day to extricate the sole occupant of each, but Robert, like his father, was methodical and patient.

Slow, Erica said to herself.

'How will you get the caterpillars to go in?' she asked.

'Ha! I'll put that down the bottom of the leaf where that join the stalk, and them old caterpillars'll walk right in.'

'But why should they?' Erica said, 'when they can stay outside and eat the cabbage?'

She could see from his slowly startled expression that this had not occurred to him before.

'Bait,' he said, at last.

'What'll you use – cheese?'

'Lettuce,' Robert said, scornfully. 'That's for caterpillars, not mice.'

'But they're Cabbage Whites, aren't they?'

'How'd you know?'

'Because you don't get other sorts on cabbages. And Cabbage White'll only want cabbage, not lettuce. They aren't Lettuce Whites. I don't know why you just don't go out and shoot them.'

'Four-eyes,' said Robert, convinced that anything his townee cousin knew about wildlife must be wrong, and curled his lip. He curled it slowly, of course. Erica was reminded of a

59

bit of bacon, rolling up under the grill. 'They'll maybe want to try something different,' he said. There was a long silence. Erica wrote, *Dear Mum and Dad, How are you? I am well. I am having a brilliant time* ...

'Anyway,' Robert yelled, suddenly, having wished his way to a deliberate triumph, 'what d'you think mice ate before they invented cheese? What d'you think they put in mouse-traps, then? Eh?'

'Shut your noise,' said his father from the settee, his face turned terrifying by the television set. He had first seen television in the days when you had to watch it in the dark, and he still did this. The curtains were drawn against the bright summer evening, where the sun shone full in at the window and the light was switched on; four lights that grew out of a kind of maimed octopus that hung from the ceiling. The television was a coloured set, but old and huge and primitive, older than Robert (though hardly more primitive, Erica thought). It was never serviced and now functioned on two colours only, yellow and purple. People glared out of the screen, their faces a dreadful acid lemon colour, with deep lilac shadows under their eyes and chins and blinding white-gold haloes as if someone were running a high-voltage electric current through them, while mysterious figures in the background swam and struggled through a thick violet syrup. Science-fiction programmes were the hardest to watch, as many of the characters had unusually tinted complexions in the first place, and a running joke about a man with green skin rather lost its point when he came out grapefruit-tinged like all his normal human friends; but even *Songs of Praise* looked like a documentary on early life-forms gasping their way out of a primeval swamp.

Erica wrote, *There is a peacock here. It is eating everything* ... while trying to work out how to tell Mum that she was enjoying herself and at the same time let her know that she was not.

There were ominous movements on the settee. Uncle Peter was working himself up to say something. Erica waited, pen

60

poised, until he said, 'Anyone feel like going out to shut up the greenhouse?'

He was not addressing Auntie Joan. Robert, very busy with a rug hook and a pair of pliers, said, 'I can go in a minute . . .' Erica got up. 'I'll go,' she said, quite glad to leave the letter, that would not allow itself to be written, and the wild writhings on the television screen, that were like a cheap stained-glass window conjured horribly to life.

The garden was still shining with sunlight, but August, getting ready for September even now, brought cool evenings that got into the greenhouse among the tomatoes and cucumbers. Erica walked through the marrow plants, warily, feeling them rasp at her jeans, under the apple trees. Birds yelled at each other from branch to branch; somewhere along the dyke the Muscovy ducks were planning a raid. From behind a row of Swiss chard the peacock suddenly reared up, jerking its head from side to side with idiot smugness, reminding Erica of those people who always turn up on television news bulletins behind the reporter, bobbing about, grinning and waving, especially when someone has just been blown to bits. It leered at her and stepped away, swinging its hips so that the tail sashayed in its wake. With a mad cry it leaped over the fence and headed for home. Erica stood by the Swiss chard, where the peacock had stood, and wished that she too could leap over the fence and head for home, but it was half past eight and the last bus left at five.

Through the branches she could see the doorway of the greenhouse; not the greenhouse itself because, full of plants, it really was green against the green hedge, but the doorway, the upright rectangle with the dark tunnel beyond it.

She meant to walk towards it, unhook the peacock trap and lean it against the pear tree, step in and close the window at the far end, then shift the bricks that held the door open against its leather hinges and drop the latch. But the staring doorway made her think of the mouth of the alley and the San Andreas Fault leading to Howlett's yard, where Elsie skulked in his

51

cave like an industrial dwarf and the Gremlin ran about, prodding. She stood under the trees, seeing it all; Elsie's domain, like a forbidden kingdom where there was no way in without a password. This morning she had said 'Jump leads' and that had got her in; but it was Uncle Peter's password, borrowed for the occasion, and, although she could use it again, she needed one of her own. It was a place where they would have to want you enough to give you a password; when you had learned the rules, perhaps.

Slowly she moved forward to do all the things that she had meant to do before, and the peacock hawked derisively in the distance. It needed no password. It went where it pleased.

Back in the living-room a terrible primrose and purple drama unfolded on the screen. Liver-coloured blood was spilled. Erica thought of the argumentative Yerbut, put together according to Elsie out of spares, who wired things up at Polthorpe Radio Services.

She said, suddenly, 'I know of someone who could mend that.'

'Mend what?' Auntie Joan said, looking all round for damaged goods.

'Mend the telly. When I was up town today –'

'Up town? Norwich?'

'No, Polthorpe.'

'That hent a town,' Uncle Peter, Auntie Joan and Robert said, all together. It was clearly a consensus.

'That's got a town hall –'

'Mend the telly?' Uncle Peter began to rotate. 'There's nothing wrong with that.'

Erica saw that she had made a mistake. 'Well, no ... not wrong. I just thought the colour looked a bit funny.'

'Funny? I suppose that *are* a bit dark,' Uncle Peter conceded. He leaned forward and began to turn a knob at the side of the set. Very gradually, as if a winter sun was rising, the faces on the screen blushed orange, and crimson flecks danced in the shadows.

'Better as that was,' Auntie Joan advised. 'More natural.'

The screen returned to its original hue, but now a strange green shape had got in and was floating about like the bubble in a spirit-level.

'Now look what you've done,' Robert snapped. He had just tested the efficacy of his caterpillar snare with his little finger and had discovered that anything that once got in could not indeed get out.

'I never touched it,' Erica said.

'Well, you didn't have to complain, did you? No one would have touched that if you hadn't've complained. You're always in a bad mind about something.'

'I'm not! I only said I knew about someone who could mend that.'

'That don't *need* mending.'

'Never send anything to Polthorpe,' Auntie Joan said. 'Never get that back. Look at your uncle's jump leads.'

Erica wrote, *Are you missing me? I can't wait* ... She nearly added *to come home*, but Auntie Joan was on her feet, headed for the kitchen, and might see what she had written while passing. She wrote, *till I see you again*, and hoped that Mum would take the hint.

Robert was unpicking his finger from the jaws of the snare. 'She're always crabbing about something. I don't know why she don't go back to Norwich.'

Nor do I, Erica mumbled, gathering up her belongings. 'I think I'll go to bed now,' she said, aloud.

'Best you do,' Robert was chanting as she went out. 'Best you do go to bed. Best you go to bed before you do any more damage.' His abuse ended in a sharp yelp. His caterpillar snare had got him again.

Erica's bedroom was growing dark. 'That face the sea,' Auntie Joan had told her when she arrived, and it did, but between the house and the sea lay the acres of farmland and marshes ending in the Marram Hills. Erica, seeing these on a map, had expected real hills, cliffs even, where the hungry sea had gnawed the hills away, but they had turned out to be sand-dunes and Auntie Joan had told her to stay out of them because they were full of adders. Further up the coast there was a kind of cliff at Happing, but it was made of mud, and the sea had only mumbled at it toothlessly; now there was a great long wooden fence that shut you in between the sea and the cliff.

Erica stood at the window, looking out at the eastern sky that was already stained with night. The lightships that stood out to sea along the coast spread pale fans across the darkness, three of them one after the other, while away to the left the Happing lighthouse swung its beam into the night. She had hoped that the lighthouse would be marooned in thrilling isolation on a storm-tossed rock, but it stood boringly on a green hillock, several hundred metres inland. Erica did not need to be told why, disappointed though she had been by the sight. The remains of its predecessor stood on the beach, behind the great wooden breakwater, nibbled away by the sea like a stick of rock. She stood at the window every night, pretending that she was at home on the third floor at Tasburgh Court, watching the headlights of the motor cycles as they came up the hill behind the houses across the valley; but this time she thought of different motor cycles, and wondered how long it would be before she could get back into Elsie's kingdom, Elsie's dank and greasy kingdom at the far end of the alley, beyond the San Andreas Fault.

Chapter Eight

She waited five days, until Monday, surviving the weekend
only by promising herself that on Monday she would go back
to Polthorpe, walk down the alley past the picture of the
winged man on his motor bike, step into Elsie's cave and say,
'Jump leads,' and Elsie would say . . .

She did not know what Elsie would say. She made a mental
list of all the things that Elsie might say, starting with, 'Come
in; nice to see you,' through 'Back already?' and 'You don't
hang about, do you?' to 'I can't have you under my feet all
the time,' and worst of any, 'Do you think I've got nothing
better to do all day than stand about talking to *you*?'

They had all, especially the latter remarks, been addressed
to her frequently by various people; by people at school and
by people out of school, when she went to visit *them* uninvited;
by the Crowd, sometimes, and by the bikers on the corner
when she prowled round their machines, because she was
only a girl in glasses and not a big lout in leathers. Even Dad
said such things, sometimes, when he caught her loitering.
'Oh, *E*rica,' said Mum, as if sorry that she had given her a
name that took so long to say.

65

Erica liked her name. She was almost the only person she knew who did like her own name; many of the others went to great lengths to persuade people to call them something different, although some people had names thrust upon them; like the eldest Murphy across the landing, who had started life as Terence, had become Terry, which seemed reasonable enough and a good place to stick at, then Tes. His friends at school lengthened this to Tesyboy, and then Yobyset, which was the same thing backwards, and now he was just known as Yob, which was unfortunate as he was quiet and peaceable and wanted to become a policeman. 'We're Irish, way back,' Yob said. 'If we lived in Ireland now they'd call me Spike.' Erica had thought that he sounded wistful, but then Yob did not know that it was possible to be a man named Elsie. Unlike the boy named Sue, he did not seem to mind. She could send him a postcard to console him, by telling him about Elsie – after all, he did have a bike of his own. Buying a postcard would be a good excuse for going to Polthorpe. Mrs Nudd's postcards were all pictures of the lighthouse and were likely to be stuck to something perishable.

But on Monday she decided to wait until Tuesday, in case Monday were too soon. (Back *already?*)

Monday was hot, after the weekend's rain, and all the people who had started their holidays in a thunderstorm came out in their cars, buzzing fretfully down the coast from Sheringham to Yarmouth, from beach to beach, like wasps unable to decide which rotten apple was sweetest. All day the bell on the stall was ringing for attention and Erica was kept busy foraging in the garden for all the vegetables that Auntie Joan had chalked up on the blackboard but had not yet got around to picking. Saturday's rain and Sunday's cloudy warmth had made things grow and swell. Beetroots were shouldering their way out of the earth and broad beans dangled with their toes on the ground, like criminals imperfectly hanged. In the Bramley a young marrow was hanging from quite a high branch and the peacock, still unscathed,

66

staggered drunkenly from plant to plant, bloated but unable to believe its luck, unable to stop gorging.

After one affluent lady with a caravan had stopped to buy almost everything on the stall – she was stocking up for the week, she explained – Erica had to go out and find replacements for all but the swedes, which not even affluent ladies seemed to want. As she was assembling them on the stall, Ted Hales called from across the road.

'Having a good holiday, then?'

'Oh *yes*,' Erica said. 'Great. *Brilliant.*' There was only one way to deal with people who asked if she were having a good holiday, and that was to lie. She was developing a special voice to do it in, and a special smile to do it through. She now knew what lying in your teeth meant.

'Want to see some piglets?' Ted invited her. 'Born yesterday?'

Erica thought of the young marrows, and how they had reminded her of piglets. Aside from the marrows there was almost nothing that she wanted to see less than Ted's piglets, but she knew from observation how Ted dearly loved a chat. She crossed the road.

The pigs sounded more than usually violent, close to, and Erica recalled how she had imagined them chained and fettered and stapled to concrete blocks and iron bars, while they worried at their prison walls with leathery snouts. Ted opened a door. 'Come and meet my old boar,' he said.

There were awful noises from inside. Erica hesitated. The mental film-strip of homicidal porkers was replaced by one of a bristly wild warthog with curly tusks.

'Is he loose?'

'He're in his pen,' Ted said. 'Come on in.'

Erica squinnied round the door frame. It was dark inside, and smelt as much of straw as of pig. A mucky bulk in the corner heaved threateningly. Ted slapped it on the back with reckless familiarity. 'Hup!'

The boar, who was only an enormous pig after all, rose up

on his hind legs and rested his front trotters on the wall of his pen. Ted, head and shoulders shorter, patted him in comradely fashion, and the boar swelled with pleasure.

'Tickle his tummy,' Ted suggested. 'Go on, he love having his tum tickled.'

Erica looked at the boar. He was so rangy that it was difficult to know what to aim for; he was all tum, from the chin down. She reached out an arm at shoulder height and tickled.

'You really need to *scratch* afore he feel anything,' Ted advised, and applied horny fingernails to the boar's underside. The whole pink body trembled with joy in tidal waves, and he moved his trotters up and down. Erica thought he looked incredibly like Mr Davis at school, standing up to play the piano in a singing lesson so that he could see what was going on in the back row.

There came a neglected bellow from the next shed.

'My sow, my old lady,' Ted said, fondly.

'Is she the one with the piglets?'

'Not this time. No, that's a young one,' Ted said, and gave the boar a friendly thump. The animal dropped on all fours again with a happy grunt and a shed-shaking thud.

'What's his name?' Erica asked, as they went out. She had a feeling that she would always think of him now as Mr Davis, and that she would never see the real Mr Davis again without thinking of Ted's old boar.

'Name?' said Ted. 'He hent got a name. What'd he want a name for? He don't get letters.'

They passed the old lady's shed. Erica had a vivid picture of an elderly pig in a poke bonnet and shawl, and she was glad that Ted had explained who his old lady was, or she might have been imagining that it was Ted's wife. She had never seen Mrs Hales. Maybe she did live in a shed.

The young sow and her farrow were over in a little shed of their own, near Ted's hen run.

'She don't want company,' Ted explained. 'I'll bring one out.' He reached into the shed and came back with a sharp-footed little pig wriggling in his arms. 'D'you want to hold him?'

The piglet looked uncommonly slippery, sketched with fine blond hair. 'I might drop him,' Erica said, and instead stroked the silky pink baby. He was warm and unexpectedly smooth.

'He's like Barry was, when he was new born,' Erica said.

'Barry? Friend of yours?'

'Barry Pearson, next door at home. He was like this – all soft and that – only he's black, not pink.'

'A Berkshire?' Ted said, still thinking of pigs.

'No, a baby.'

'Bet you thought he was going to be all prickly.'

'Who – Barry?'

'No, him here. People always do.'

'Yes, I did,' Erica said. She looked at the squirming infant, so very like Barry, so very like any baby. Barry Pearson was probably going to grow up to look like his dad, which couldn't be bad, but the little pig was going to grow up to look like *his* dad too, and presumably that was Mr Davis, Ted's old boar. Ted put the piglet back in its pen and closed the door, while Erica remembered that probably it was not going to grow up at all, or not very far, and wondered if she would ever be able to eat bacon again.

As she said good-bye to Ted and walked back across his yard she saw that two cars had drawn up outside Hall Farm Cottage, and there was Auntie Joan, flapping between them – like a hen with its head cut off, Erica thought, although she had never seen anything so lively. Mum had described it to her.

'*There* you are,' Auntie Joan said, as if Erica herself did not know where she was. 'Run you and pull me some carrots – two pounds with the greens off, was it, Madam?'

A voice, which was too lazy to get out of the rear car, said yes, it *was* two pounds, suggesting that if she had to wait any longer it wouldn't be anything at all. Erica hurried to the carrot rows, but not too quickly, hating the voice for making

Auntie Joan run about for it, and furious with Auntie Joan for running about and saying Madam. It wasn't as if she were even in a proper shop, Erica thought. She could not imagine Elsie calling anyone Madam. She ripped the innocent carrots from the earth and scalped them by twisting their topknots.

In the distance she saw furtive movement and thought it was the peacock; then she realized that it was Robert, carefully keeping out of sight, and she was so enraged that without meaning to she twisted a carrot in two, like someone showing off with a beer can.

When she returned with the carrots, weighed in the garage and wrapped in an old *Eastern Daily Press*, the first car had gone and the second was grumbling impatiently. Auntie Joan took the carrots and passed them in at the passenger window. No one inside the car said anything, although Erica saw several fat faces staring out, but Auntie Joan said 'Thank you, Madam,' and stepped back to allow the car to sweep away. She would have had to step back in any case, to avoid being run over, but she managed to make it look polite rather than prudent.

Then she turned to Erica.

'Where've you been?'

'I was over at Ted's, meeting his old boar,' Erica said.

'I thought you was supposed to be sorting out the stall.'

'I did – then Ted called . . .'

'I thought you was serving. I was out the other side, getting the washing in. I didn't know you wasn't here until I heard the horns.'

'Horns?'

'Hooters. The cars. They was blowing their hooters. To call me out,' Auntie Joan said. She was clearly indignant and not worried about making a guest feel uncomfortable. 'I've never had people *queuing* before.'

'That was only two of them,' Erica protested.

'Yes, but they wanted more than I'd got, didn't they? They both wanted carrots. And where was you?'

'Couldn't Robert have pulled them?' Erica asked, unwisely, as Robert looked over the hedge with skeins of bast and old fruit netting over his arm, probably destined to become a trap of some kind.

'I were busy,' Robert said, calmly.

'Didn't *you* hear the hooters?' Erica asked him. 'I'd have thought –'

'That's none of your business whether he heard or not. I asked *you* to help. You said you would. If you didn't want to you should have *said* –'

'But I did want to. I like doing that.'

'That don't make any difference whether you like that or not. If you say you'll do a thing, you *do* that.'

'But I *was*!' Erica wailed. 'And then Ted called over did I want to come and see his piglets, and then he showed me his old boar.'

'If you ask me, Ted's an old bore,' Robert observed.

Erica waited for Auntie Joan to reprimand him for this piece of rudeness, but Robert still was not in the firing line. Erica was.

'You hent to sneak out unless you tell me where you're going.'

Erica realized that Auntie Joan probably had been worried about her, but she was too angered by being bawled out in front of idle Robert to give her credit for it. She stalked into the garden, followed by idle Robert.

'You got wrong there,' he said, placidly. He had not forgiven her for being the indirect cause of the mysterious green bubble in the television set, which had stopped drifting from side to side and was now given to wandering mazily like a bathysphere with a drunken driver.

'Why should I have to do all the running about while you just slob around and turn old rubbish into more old rubbish?' Erica shouted. 'What're you going to do with that lot – build a marrow trap?'

Robert paused, puzzled. 'A marrow trap?' he asked, seriously. 'What for? Marrows don't have pests.'

'I meant a trap to catch marrows,' Erica said, seeing him thoroughly fazed. 'You could make it like those eel traps I saw in the museum. You know, wide one end and getting narrower and you chase the marrows in and they can't get out again. Then you bap them, just like eels. Then you get a big knife and slit their throats aaaaaaaaaaargh! An' there's green marrow blood everywhere.'

'You're off your head,' Robert said, slowly but with conviction. 'Marrow's hent got throats.'

'Or blood,' he added, several seconds later.

Erica shrugged and walked away. She had been considering, for a moment, inviting him to share a joke, but she knew it would be useless. Robert's jokes came out of comics and joke-books, ready pre-packaged. He would never believe that anything you just *said* could be a joke. Erica's plans for the marrow traps weren't a joke, just loopy talk.

It struck her that Robert would be lost in Elsie's kingdom. He would not understand it because he would not want to understand it, and because he would never know that he did not understand.

She tested him next morning. When she awoke to the sound of the peacock being slaughtered she got up, instead of sulking under the bedclothes, and went downstairs. To atone for yesterday's dereliction of duty, she picked armfuls of vegetables and set up the stall, with its bell, before anyone else was about. She and the peacock had the garden to themselves, but they'd nothing against each other and picked peas harmoniously, side by side. When she was washing up after breakfast, leaving Auntie Joan to discover the stall and be decently delighted, or something like it, and Robert was settled at the table with his marrow trap, she said casually:

'I thought I'd go out on the Iron Cow today.'

'The what?'

'The Iron Cow,' Erica said, 'over the San Andreas Fault ... past Copernicus ...' She still was not too sure who Copernicus could be – possibly the dentist – but Robert had no idea at all what she was talking about.

'Why don't you talk straight?' was all he said, and Erica knew that he would never have a password, and never follow her into Elsie's kingdom.

Chapter Nine

All she needed now was the loan of the Iron Cow and permission to go into Polthorpe. The prospect looked promising, for Auntie Joan was pleased about the stall, although not *wildly* pleased, but there was a chance that she would herself have plans for the Iron Cow; and Robert would never allow Erica to lay a hand on his own machine, although Erica, having seen him on it, knew that she was the better cyclist. Robert, for a start, rode mainly on the right and had only one hand signal, a kind of dangling floppy gesture as if he were trailing his fingers in the water over the side of a boat.

When Auntie Joan returned from delivering Beth Nudd's order, and Robert was out of sight in the garden staking out his nets, which now looked like an assault course for hedgehogs, Erica hurried up and down the stairs several times to give the impression that she was really very busy, and then looked in briefly at the kitchen door, saying, 'Would you like me to go to Polthorpe for you?'

'Polthorpe?' Auntie Joan said. 'Whatever for?'

Erica felt discouraged. No one at Hall Farm Cottage ever went anywhere without a very good reason. Energy con-

74

servation took on a whole new meaning here, Erica thought.

'I could go and see if the leads were ready.'

'Leads?'

'Uncle Peter's jump leads – at Els – at Mercury Bikes.' She felt suddenly very shy about mentioning Elsie, as if she were in danger of giving away something without meaning to.

'Oh, them. Yes. You might as well. What else could you do while you're there?' Auntie Joan asked, worriedly, afraid that Erica might waste time; time better used, Erica added nastily to herself, in making toad traps. Auntie Joan was staring thoughtfully out of the window. 'You could take him some marrows.'

'Who?' Erica's schedule for the morning had not included marrows.

'Elsie. He might like a marrow. In fact,' Auntie Joan said, her list growing audibly longer, 'you could take a whole load. Ask if anyone else is interested. There's a whole lot of them in that yard.'

'Yes, there are,' Erica thought, horrified. Elsie and Bunny and Yerbut and Jack and Bill Birdcycles, and Alan and Alan's old lady and the Gremlin, Kermit, Kermit's Karen ... and they were just the ones she knew about.

'You go out and see what's fit,' Auntie Joan said. 'I'll bring the bike round and set that up.'

Erica went back into the garden. What was fit was marrows and swedes; bulking things with no angles to grasp.

'Where're you taking them marrows?' Robert asked, draped in fruit netting under the trees like the clever girl in the fairy tale who was told to come neither naked nor clothed and turned up in a fishing net.

'You took my advice then,' Erica said.

'I never,' Robert snapped. He had no idea which advice she meant, but he was sure that he had not taken any.

'You're making marrow traps,' Erica pointed out.

'Don't be soft. This is to stop the old cats sharpening their claws on them.'

75

'On the marrows? There aren't any cats,' Erica said. Auntie Joan and Uncle Peter would never countenance the presence of a cat in the house; cats were a waste of time and floor space and were well known to be infested with fleas, tics and tapeworms.

'There might be,' Robert said, presciently. 'There weren't no peacock this time last year, and now look.'

When she had carted her cargo back to the house she discovered what Auntie Joan had meant about setting up the bike. As well as the freezer basket on the handlebars it now carried a small seat behind the saddle, also cast iron and upholstered in shiny black oilcloth.

'Used to carry Robert in that,' Auntie Joan said, fondly. 'And my mum used to carry me, but that weren't new when she got it. Found that on a bomb site in Yarmouth.'

'Is that where she found the bike?' Erica asked, unsure if it were safe to make jokes about the Iron Cow to Auntie Joan, but Auntie Joan took her seriously.

'Oh no, that belonged to *my* gran.' Auntie Joan was packing vegetables into the freezer basket. 'You know the price. Knock off tuppence a pound and make that twenty p. for the marrows.'

'You've left the marrows out,' Erica said, but then saw why. There were five of them. Auntie Joan was propping them upright in the baby seat above the rear mudguard.

'They'll fall out,' Erica said hopelessly, able only too clearly to imagine herself creaking along the lanes to Polthorpe with the marrows jostling at her back like recalcitrant quintuplets. What would the boy at the council houses yell this time?

'No they won't,' Auntie Joan said, and made sure of it by buckling a strap round the middles of the marrows, trussing the five of them together like monstrous sticks of gelignite. The marrows had no more waists than did Ted's old boar, but they seemed securely enough fixed.

The Iron Cow was now dangerously overloaded. Auntie Joan wheeled it out into the road and held it steady, while

76

Erica climbed in, levered herself onto the saddle and started to turn the pedals. She began to see why bicycles were referred to as machines. It seemed impossible that so much effort should not produce a finished article, or at least, as the boy at the council houses had suggested, milk. She supposed that a cow was really a kind of milk machine.

As she rode away towards Calstead Corner she heard Auntie Joan shouting, perhaps a farewell, perhaps a warning or just an instruction, but turning her head even slightly shifted her centre of gravity and the Iron Cow bucked in a threatening way.

Negotiating bends was going to be thoroughly dangerous. Erica, turning Calstead Corner at a stately wobble, remembered the flattened cucumber and was haunted thereafter by the prospect of the marrows leaping overboard and hurling themselves suicidally under the wheels of passing vehicles.

The boy from the council houses was not in his garden to shout at her today, but just beyond she met Ted, riding very slowly in the opposite direction.

'Taking them to market?' he asked. Erica nodded. She dared not turn her head, she could not even raise her hand from the handlebars to wave. She just nodded and hoped that Ted would guess why and not think her rude.

She knew what he had meant when she got to Polthorpe. Polthorpe Street was half a mile long from start to finish, and today it was ravelled with traffic jams at regular intervals, like knots in cotton. There were no artics about this morning, but every few yards a van unloading or a car making a right-hand turn brought everything to a halt. At either end a bus waited, stoically. It must be market day.

Erica could not imagine where the market might be. In Norwich the market was open all week, on the great plain below City Hall; it was there all the time, it even had its own refuse collections, and when the stall-holders packed up and went home, the stalls remained. When she had got rid of the marrows, she decided, she might go and look for Polthorpe market, although if the industrial estate were anything to go by it would probably turn out to be two stalls and a litter bin.

It was impossible to ride up the Street and remain vertical, so slow was the pace. Erica climbed down from the Iron Cow, took it by the horns and guided it in and out of snarled-up traffic, round reversing cars and up onto the pavement to collide dangerously with oncoming perambulators. She was very aware of her pillion passengers, but no one took any notice of the marrows. Presumably Auntie Joan was simply observing a well-established custom, and this was the normal way to carry your goods to market. Did pigs travel by bike as well?

Outside Marsh's a fish van was drawn up across the mouth of the alley, where the owner and a potential customer were wrangling over a fillet of cod. A notice was propped against the nearside wing, advertising what was for sale. Erica noticed squid near the bottom of the list and glanced into the back of the van, hoping to see writhing tentacles, but it was only full of ordinary flat white fish and freckled plaice, and yellow smoked haddock like something out of Auntie Joan's television set. On the floor were plastic buckets of cockles and mussels. Erica wondered if the fishmonger would consider bartering a marrow for a pint of mussels, but the cod war was reaching strategic proportions, so carefully manoeuvring the Iron Cow she threaded her way between the combatants and into the alley.

The yard was transformed. Last week she had called in at nine o'clock; now it was half past ten and the estate had become industrious if not industrial. The two or three vans had multiplied to a dozen, and outside Elsie's cave the row of bikes awaiting his attention had lengthened noticeably. Elsie himself was in the doorway talking to a man, and Bunny's lugubrious bulk could be seen in the dark hinterland, moving to and fro.

Neither Elsie nor his companion noticed her as she parked the Iron Cow in the fireweed, its natural habitat. She hovered.

78

After a while the man turned to leave, saw her and said, 'You got a customer, Elsie.'

Erica held her breath. Elsie turned round and said, 'Ah, the Cow with the Crumpled Horn.'

'You don't have to take any lip from him,' Bunny said, looming darkly over Elsie's shoulder. 'Cow with the Crumpled Horn, indeed. Hit him in the eye.'

'I didn't mean you,' Elsie said, to Erica.

'I know,' Erica said. 'That's the bike. I call that the Iron Cow.'

'As good a handle as any,' said Elsie. 'Now, what can I do you for?'

'Jump leads,' Erica said. The password.

'Oh god,' said Elsie. 'Hang about.' He turned and plunged into the Cave. Erica followed him.

'I'm Erica. Erica Timperley.'

She had hoped that he would instantly transform that into a handle too. It seemed that you needed a handle here, as well as a password, and it struck her as rather unfair that the bicycle should have a handle while she had only a name. She wondered if she could invent her own or if it had to be bestowed by someone else, and whether, once she had it, it would take immediately or have to be grown into slowly, like a school coat. The telephone rang on its shelf.

Elsie, who had evidently forgotten all about the jump leads until she reminded him, was back in his burrow under the bench, and Bunny emerged from an oily recess beneath the clouded window to answer it. He had some trouble getting into the booth and was forced to insinuate himself sideways, then make a three-point turn until he was facing the shelf where the telephone stood. The shelf was so stacked with papers that he could not find the telephone at all, and had to scrabble among dirty rags and invoices. Elsie, from under the bench, called out, 'Hey, Bunny, answer it, will you?'

A pile of old ledgers hit the floor. Bunny still could not find the telephone although Erica, on the other side of the glass, could see it quite plainly. She went over and pointed. Bunny swept aside a drift of letters and located the handset as a lithe and hairy spider leaped out of the mouthpiece. Bunny, who had had his hand on the receiver, would have jumped back, but he so filled the booth that there was no room for him to move any way at all. Instead he swelled sideways, out of the doorway, never taking his eyes from the spider, his hand still gripping the receiver and the telephone still ringing. He groaned, faintly.

Elsie looked over the top of the counter, just his eyes showing, like Chad. 'For crying out loud, Bunny, are you going to answer it or not?' Bunny burst out of the doorway so violently that the booth seemed to implode behind him. The spider was jiving up his arm. Bunny was running too, with great thumps, out into the yard. Erica put her arm round the door of the booth and retrieved the handset which was now hanging by its cord. An angry voice at the other end of the line said, 'What the *hell* are you doing, Elsie? Having a bath?'

'Who is it?' Elsie said, vaulting over the counter. He came down with one foot in a can of Swarfega which had been left negligently on the floor.

'Someone wants to know if you're having a bath.'

'I am now,' Elsie said, equably, with his shoe still in the can. He withdrew his foot, leaving the shoe engulfed, and hopped over to the booth.

'Are you *dead*, Elsie?' the voice inquired, nastily.

'He's just coming.'

'He'd better be.'

Elsie reached the booth and took the receiver from Erica. 'Hullo?'

The earpiece was now clamped to the side of Elsie's head but the voice, like a berserk wasp in a jam jar, still reached Erica. Tactfully she took herself outside to where Bunny was gyrating strangely in the fireweed.

'That's a phobia,' he explained, sheepishly, as Erica tiptoed up behind him.

'I thought that was a spider,' Erica said.

'I'm not really frightened of them,' Bunny said. 'I just can't *stand* them.'

Erica thought that this came to much the same thing. 'That's on your back,' she said.

'Get that off,' Bunny begged her. '*Can* you?' he added, doubtfully. Erica, feeling smug, dropped her curved palm over the spider, withdrew it and held it out for him to admire. Bunny seemed to shrink several inches inward and the ribs on his T-shirt went into accordion pleats.

'They don't hurt,' Erica said. 'I mean, that's not like tarantulas and black widows and Mexican red-knees –'

'Shut up!'

'English spiders don't bite.'

'You can never tell which way they're going to run – all those legs,' Bunny said, nervously. 'With eight to choose from they could go anywhere.'

'I like them,' Erica said, with callous satisfaction.

Elsie came out, rubbing his head where the telephone wasp had been etching at his ear.

'Who was it?' Bunny asked.

'I should have thought that was the least of your problems,' Elsie said. 'You had a chance to find out but your mind was on other things.'

'There was a spider in the phone.'

'I thought there was one up your nose, after that performance,' Elsie said.

'Here it is,' Erica said, showing him her cupped hands. The spider waved a leg suggestively through a crack between two fingers.

'What are you going to do with it – teach it tricks?' Elsie asked. 'Train it to fetch things? The world's only retrieving spider.'

'My dad used to do that with my auntie's cat,' Bunny said. 'He used to throw fag ends in the fire and shout "Fetch!" But that never did. He hated that old cat, it used to nest in his hat. Do get rid of that thing – what'syourname? Erica.'

Here was a chance for Elsie to come in again with a better handle, but he was still thinking about the telephone. 'It was a message for old Arrow,' he said. He handed a piece of paper to Bunny. 'Take it up to him, will you?'

'Why?' Bunny demanded, trying to look truculent.

'Because you're nearer than I am.'

'By about six inches,' Bunny said, but he tweaked the note out of Elsie's fingers and took off slowly across the yard, fingering the back of his neck as if he suspected that the spider might have left an accomplice behind to carry on with the good work.

Chapter Ten

Elsie and Erica walked back to the Cave, and it seemed quite natural, as if she belonged there.

'You're not going to put that thing back in the phone, are you?' Elsie said.

'What thing?'

'Your little friend with the legs. I should leave it out here if I were you.'

'Oh, that.' Erica opened her hands and tipped the spider into the fireweed, where it flexed its many limbs tentatively, like an athlete afraid of muscle strain. Immediately the stalks parted and out came the ancient black and white cat with the false teeth. She watched the spider shortsightedly, her head on one side, and began to go after it, sharp elbows arthritically akimbo; but the spider was faster.

'*Fetch*, Panda,' Elsie said, as predator and prey disappeared into the fireweed, just as Bunny's dad had done to his auntie's cat.

'Is that her real name?' Erica asked, 'or another handle?'

'Her name is Puddypaws,' Elsie pronounced, his mouth wry with distaste. 'Would you want to be called Puddypaws? She comes from the pet shop but they keep her out of sight because she's a bad advertisement. She used to sit on the hamster cage and dribble. People objected to paying for damp hamsters. Anyway, with a phiz like that she has to be Panda.'

'A phiz?'

'Physiognomy. Face,' Elsie said.

'Why's Bunny called Bunny, then?' Erica asked, picturing Bunny's very human phiz.

'He's been Bunny since school,' Elsie said. 'So they tell me. I didn't know him at school. His real name's Bernard.'

Erica wanted to say, 'And what's yours?' but it was different from asking about someone else; ruder. Anyway, she knew what his real name was; what she wanted to know was why he was called Elsie.

Elsie had seen the Iron Cow's passengers. 'Now there's a kind thought,' he said.

'What?'

'Taking your auntie's marrows for a ride. They'll appreciate that. Marrows are generally fairly ill-educated – they ought to be encouraged to broaden their horizons. They don't read much either,' he added. 'Just magazine stories, mostly, and romantic fiction.'

Erica thought of Mr Davis, Ted's old boar who didn't get letters. 'Auntie Joan wanted me to try and sell them.'

'Sell them? Here?'

Erica looked at her feet. If she had been Elsie, busy with welding and motor cycles and telephone calls and Swarfega, she would not have welcomed a stranger who turned up with marrows riding pillion on the back of a bicycle. She saw herself again a stranger.

'Who are you going to sell them to?'

Erica looked up at him. He was not so very much taller than she was, and she stood close enough to see that he was amused and not offended that she had come into his kingdom to flog vegetables.

'*I don't know*,' she said. 'I never wanted to bring them. I'm

84

sorry – it's not my fault. I just told Auntie Joan that I'd see if the leads were ready, and she said to bring along some vegetables and see if anybody wanted them. I don't know who to ask and the leads aren't ready, are they?' She would have to return to Calstead leadless, with the freezer basket still loaded and the marrows still sitting stolidly in the seat behind. She also observed that Elsie looked very shifty every time leads were mentioned.

'Tell you what,' he said. 'If I put one of our tables outside the door, you could set up a stall. You never know, someone might want something. We get a lot of people in and out.'

'Bikers?'

'No, not bikers,' Elsie said. 'There aren't any bikers round here except Yerbut's brother and he has to go on the bus since he smashed up his Suzuki. He still wears his leathers, though. He carries his helmet in a string bag,' said Elsie.

'What's his – handle?'

'Fang,' Elsie said.

'Fang – like Dracula?'

'That's right. He's only got two of his own. He's one of those statistics you read about; people who have a complete set of false choppers by the time they're twenty-one.'

'Not a complete set,' Erica argued. 'You said he had two of his own.'

'He's only twenty, yet,' Elsie said. 'What else could we call him, Goldilocks?'

'Has he got fair hair?'

'Not noticeably,' Elsie said. 'Not noticeably hair at all, as it happens.' Yerbut's brother was obviously a youth of advanced decrepitude. 'Come on, give me a hand with this table.'

The table was just behind the left-hand leaf of the double doors. It was, like just about every other flat surface in the Cave, piled with oily rags, but Elsie swept them magnificently to the floor, saying, 'It's Bunny's turn to sweep up today,' and they carried it outside, one at each end.

85

'Do you have a CB?' Erica asked.

'Fat chance,' Elsie said. 'Why d'you ask?'

'All these handles.'

'Names were handles long before CB got on the road,' Elsie said. 'People have always gone after names that suited them better than their own. Calling yourself Englebert Bottleneck or the Long Range Ferret and clogging up the frequencies doesn't make you any more exciting just because you have a tachograph instead of a brain.' He looked almost surly.

'You made them up,' Erica accused him.

'On my mother's grave ...' Elsie said, crossing his heart, 'wherever that may turn out to be, she's good for a few years yet. Would you believe the Lonesome Turnip?'

'No.'

'I pick him up on my hi-fi. Lonesome Turnip and I are going to lock horns if we ever cross wavelengths, as it were. He should be fairly easy to recognize, don't you think?'

They stood the table between the row of motor cycles and the fireweed. Elsie helped to unpack the swedes while Erica freed the marrows from their restraining strap and arranged them like Stonehenge, three standing up and two along the top, at the back of the display, leaning against the wall.

'Right,' Elsie said. 'There you are. All you need now is customers. Step inside and have a cup of tea.'

'Suppose someone comes?'

'They'll yell. Hadn't you noticed?'

Erica followed him into the Cave. Among the tools and machines on the counter was an electric kettle plugged into a serpentine extension lead which wandered all over the floor in expansive loops, before disappearing under the bench not far from where the kettle stood. Erica realized that she had her own password, after all. 'Jump leads' would get her in, but so would 'Marrows'. All she needed now was a handle.

By eleven thirty Erica had drunk two cups of tea and nipped across the road for sausage rolls, and Elsie still had not found the leads. His current method of searching was to change the positions of all the objects on top of the bench, and Erica was quite relieved on his behalf when a customer came in and let him off the hook.

There was a strange gibbering in the alley outside, like a steel fork beating eggs in a tin jug.

'Kevin's Fizzy,' Elsie remarked, without looking up to see if he were right.

'Who shook him up then?' Erica said.

'I'm talking about his bike,' Elsie said.

'Yamaha F S 1 E,' Erica said. 'I know what a Fizzy is. And I know what *that* is,' she said, pointing to the frame on the oil cans. 'That's an Indian.'

Elsie looked at her with some respect.

'You've seen one before?'

'I've seen pictures,' Erica said. 'I've always wanted to meet a real one. What are you doing with it?'

'Restoring it,' Elsie said, with a fanatical look in his eye. Erica could tell from that and from the tone of his voice that he was delighted to meet a fellow worshipper, but before they could say any more, and just as she was about to ask him where he had found it, Kevin appeared in the doorway.

'What's up today?' Elsie said. Kevin was plainly a regular customer.

Kevin came out of his helmet. 'Sounds a bit rough,' he said apologetically, as if he were complaining of a sore throat and thought that he was making a fuss about nothing. 'Lacking power.'

'All Fizzies sound a bit rough,' Elsie said, 'and yours sounds like an eggbeater. Let's have a look. Man the telephone will you, Erica, if it rings.' Erica stayed in the Cave but hovered in the doorway, partly in case Kevin fancied buying a marrow, and partly because she wanted to go on listening to Elsie, who had thought exactly the same as she had about the Yamaha's engine.

Kevin had left his Fizzy on the end of the queue of bikes.

87

He looked at the length of the queue. 'You got a lot on?' he asked, dolefully.

'I'm working through them,' Elsie said. 'There's nothing major except for Freddie's Honda,' he pointed to a very bent machine, halfway along, 'but then Freddie's a bit dented too. He's in no hurry.'

'Went into a bus, didn't he?' Kevin said.

'Not precisely *into* it,' Elsie said, 'but right down one side. The bike's in a mess, but you should have seen the bus. When do you need yours?'

'I got a job interview on Thursday,' Kevin said. 'In Yarmouth. I'll need that for that.'

'I don't see why not, but wouldn't you stand a better chance if you went on the bus and wore a suit?'

'I haven't got one,' Kevin said.

'Anything's better than jeans and Doctor Martens. Particularly those jeans.'

'I'll take my old school trousers and change in the gents,' said Kevin.

'I wish you luck,' Elsie said, without much expectancy in his voice. 'Well, leave it with me and drop in tomorrow. I don't expect it'll be anything serious – or expensive,' he went on, kindly. 'You don't want to buy a marrow, do you?'

'Not a lot,' Kevin said.

'They're only twenty pence,' said Elsie. Erica had not expected Elsie to do her marketing for her. Anxious to back him up she hefted the sleekest marrow and held it out for Kevin's inspection.

'That's fresh,' she said.

Kevin rapped it with his knuckles and it thrummed soundly.

'All right,' he said, unexpectedly, and took it, holding out two tenpenny pieces. Erica was about to accept them when Elsie's oily mitt was interposed.

'Come back about ten tomorrow,' he said, chucking the coins in his hand.

'Cheers,' said Kevin, and left on foot. Erica looked anxiously at Elsie's fist. He went back into the Cave, opened his cash box and put the money in. He took out a handful of copper, counted it carefully, and handed Erica nineteen pence, one penny at a time.

'Nineteen for you,' he said, 'and one for me. We're in business, yes?'

'Oh, yes!' Erica said as her hand closed over the money, feeling obscurely more pleased to receive nineteen pence from Elsie than twenty from Kevin.

'If you make the sale,' he said, 'you keep it all. If I make the sale I get a penny commission. When I've saved a pound, we'll celebrate.'

'But there's not enough out there,' Erica said. 'You'll not make 10p.'

'Well, bring some more tomorrow,' said Elsie, and Erica could hardly believe that she had heard him correctly, but she was afraid to ask him to repeat it in case she had not.

Back across the yard came Bunny, treading carefully and looking at the ground as if he suspected that his spider might be lying in wait, hoping to finish the job this time.

'Over your arachniphobia?' Elsie inquired.

'Me what?'

'Morbid and irrational fear of spiders ... and work,' Elsie said. 'Old Arrow must be all of thirty seconds' walk from here. What did you do – make a detour round King's Lynn?'

'Stayed for a chat and had a look at his back boiler,' Bunny said, with dignity. 'Ah, his soldered joints are a picture ... You, of course, have been working your fingers to the bone while I was away, stirring teacups and switching on kettles –'

'*Which* reminds me,' Elsie interrupted, 'next time you switch the kettle on, use an insulated screwdriver. I drew sparks just now. Fancy a little job now that you're rested?'

'Kevin's Fizzy,' Bunny said. 'I heard it. What's wrong with that this time?'

'That's what you're going to find out,' Elsie said. 'Take

89

it for a run and see what you think. *I* think the best thing he can do is take the engine out and boil it.'

Bunny went into the Cave, returned with a crash helmet and swung his heavy leg over Kevin's Fizzy. He saw the marrows and the swedes. 'Going into the vegetable trade, are we?'

'Me and my partner here,' Elsie said. 'I shall expect you to support us. Buy a marrow, why don't you?'

'Why should I?' Bunny said, as the two-stroke clattered into action.

' 'Cause I'll thump you if you don't!' Elsie bawled. Bunny made a rude sign and wheeled the machine towards the mouth of the alley at exactly the moment someone on another bike entered from the far end. Erica could not see who it was, but Elsie's fine-tuned ear was pricked.

'Kermit!' he cried, and wrapped his arms round his head in readiness for the collision that was coming. 'Crash, grind, rip, tinkle-tinkle-tinkle ...' At the last minute Bunny swung the Fizzy to one side and Kermit roared out of the alley on his Honda, with the Gremlin mounted behind him in a very small crash helmet.

'That could have been messy,' Elsie remarked, emerging from the shelter of his forearms. 'Oh God, the Gremlin. Here we go; prod, prod. He'll be after your marrows, Erica. He won't be able to resist them.'

The Gremlin climbed down and cantered in the direction of the chippy to collect his special prodding stick. Kermit raised a gauntleted arm and moved off again.

'He's cool,' Elsie said. 'In the face of death he's cool, man, is he cool? But he's a coward at heart.'

'How d'you know?' Erica said.

'If he weren't a coward he'd have stopped here for a chat but he was afraid of what I'd say about him dumping the Gremlin.' He went into the Cave, shaking his head. 'No moral fibre. No moral fibre at all.'

*

90

'What's the time?' Erica said.

'Twelve thirty. Soon as Bunny comes back – where the hell has he got to this time, I don't know what he thinks I pay him for, he was only supposed to be trying the damn thing out – as I was saying when I was so rudely interrupted, when Bunny comes back, *if* he comes back, which I'm beginning to doubt, I'll knock off for lunch.'

'I'd better get home.' Erica had not noticed how time was passing. You never did, somehow, when you were having a good time. It was like maths lessons at school, which passed almost before she had time to enjoy them, while English and cookery crept like slugs across the timetable. 'Auntie Joan thinks I only came for the leads and the marrows.'

'Well, you've been selling marrows,' Elsie said, ignoring the reference to leads. They had sold three marrows, one to Uncle Alan from the chippy, who had not wanted it but who had been threatened with the mysterious disappearance of the Gremlin if he refused to buy, and who gave it to the Gremlin to prod.

'I'm only doing this as a favour,' he said. 'You can disappear him any time you like. That's fine by me.'

Erica said, 'Can I leave the rest here and come back after lunch?'

'Why not?' Elsie said. 'We'll get the sign changed; *Mercury Marrows. Purveyor of Gourds to the Gentry.*'

'Thanks ever so for selling them,' Erica said. 'That's ever so nice of you.'

'I've made three pence, so far,' Elsie reminded her.

'Can I help with the bikes?' Erica said, daringly, 'as you're helping with the marrows?'

'What d'you mean, help?' Elsie said suspiciously. 'Not prodding?'

'No!' Erica was indignant. 'Proper doing. I can see to the Fizzy.'

'You don't know what's wrong with it.'

Erica was tugging the Iron Cow out of the fireweed. 'I bet that's the exhaust. I bet that is.'

91

'Why?'

'Because that's a two-stroke. I bet the exhaust port's full of gunge.'

'I bet it's the carb,' Elsie said, contrarily, 'also full of gunge. All right, you're on. If it's the exhaust you can have the three pence back.'

'What if that's the carb?' Erica was shouting down the alley.

'You can clean it out!' Elsie shouted after her. 'There, that way you can't lose!'

Chapter Eleven

There was going to be trouble when she got home. She could feel it developing all the way along the Calstead road, past the Methodist Chapel, rising out of the ground as the mist did in the evenings; so when she rounded Calstead Corner and saw Hall Farm Cottage with Auntie Joan standing in the road outside, she was worried, but not surprised. The worry was situated halfway down and somewhere near her middle, dark and flattened like a second liver.

Auntie Joan was standing exactly as people do in pictures when they stare out to sea, leaning forward slightly, with one hand shielding her eyes from the sun. She was standing dangerously far out into the road, too, as if being run down from behind was a small price to pay for seeing Erica come safely home.

Erica urged the Iron Cow into a canter and tried to look as if she had been riding very fast all the way home instead of dawdling to ward off the trouble for just a little longer.

'You heard me call you when you went,' Auntie Joan said as she drew level. 'You heard me tell you back by eleven thirty.'

'I never.' Erica risked an outright lie in the interests of simplicity.

'I were going to call the police,' Auntie Joan announced flatly. 'I thought you'd had an accident. I thought someone had made off with you.'

'I've been selling marrows,' Erica said.

'You're always hearing about young girls who disappear while they're out on their bikes,' Auntie Joan went on, remorselessly. If she really had been worried she was not going to let the worry go to waste. 'I expected you back by half-past eleven.'

'I've only been at – at – Mercury Bikes,' Erica said. 'Really.'

'For three hours? How could I know where you were?' Auntie Joan complained, grabbing the Iron Cow's crumpled horn as if she were afraid it would career off on its own. 'I've been in and out of this gate looking for you. Did you get the leads? Where's the vegetables?'

'We're selling them,' Erica said. 'Honestly. I'm going back after lunch.'

'Who say you're going back after lunch?' Auntie Joan was properly angry, not just putting it on, as Mum did, because she thought she ought to. 'You don't mean to tell me you've left them there? Where did you leave them?'

'That's only two marrows and the swedes,' Erica said. 'Nobody wants the swedes, but we're selling the marrows.'

They went wrangling indoors.

'Three *hours* to sell three *marrows*? *Who's* selling them?'

'Me and Elsie.' That sounded good. 'We've put up a table outside the Cave – shop – and people are buying. They *are*. Elsie takes a penny commission every time he sells something. So I've got fifty-seven pence,' Erica said.

'And he've got three?'

'Yes.' Erica sensed that it might be unwise to hint that there might be a chance of winning them back.

'Off of our marrows?'

'That's only fun,' Erica said.

'That'd better be.'

'I *planted* them marrows,' Robert said, glowering at the table. Erica was staggered to think that he had ever planted anything. 'That ought to be *my* 3p.'

Erica put the fifty-seven pence on the table. Elsie had used their partnership as an excuse to clear out his loose change. During the couple of hours that Erica had spent in the Cave, most of the bills presented had been in round figures, but people tended to use Elsie as an excuse to clear out *their* loose change. There were two fivepenny pieces, ten twopences, thirteen pennies and twenty-eight halfpennies which, Elsie maintained, had been clogging up his works for weeks.

Robert looked at the rising columns with disapproval. Money, in his opinion, was not for playing with.

'That smell of petrol,' he said.

'That do,' Auntie Joan chimed in at once. 'Now get that off of the table – we've been waiting lunch for you.'

Erica swept the money into her palm. Having lunch kept waiting for you was almost worse than being kept waiting for lunch. You felt guilty as well as hungry. 'But I can go back after?' she said. 'And sell the rest? I could take some carrots and that. That's a proper stall – like yours.'

'And what'll they say at Hobson's?' Hobson was one of the greengrocers. 'When Tuddenham's started selling potatoes they put up a notice. *We* don't sell newspapers, it said.'

Erica visualized an angry sign outside the greengrocery: *We do not sell motor cycles.* She looked down at the table where Auntie Joan was setting a tureen of mashed swedes and a bowl of boiled marrow. It would have been silly to expect anything else, really.

'I'll tell you a good selling line,' Elsie said. 'Personalized marrows. People will have to book them in advance of course, but you could do a roaring trade with the tourists: A PRESENT FROM POLTHORPE! COME TO SUNNY CALSTEAD FOR YOUR HOLIDAY OF A LIFETIME!'

'What *are* you on about?' Bunny asked, plaintively. He was removing the carb from Kevin's Fizzy, preparatory to deciding whether Elsie or Erica had won the bet, of which proceeding he deeply disapproved. Erica and Elsie, who had taken time off from his everyday duties to work on the Indian's engine, leaned over anxiously to watch.

'Don't tell me you've never written on a marrow,' Elsie said. 'You haven't lived! And you were *born* here, in the heart of marrow country. Fields of marrows, swaying in the breeze, marrow refineries, herds of merry yokels swigging squash wine to celebrate the marrow harvest, all the wains are draped with marrow vines and the young girls have marrow flowers in their hair. Marrows even grow on trees, round here.'

'They do, too,' Erica said. 'Come on, Bunny, get the fuel bowl off.'

'Who are you Bunnying?' Bunny growled.

'She can call you Bunny if she likes, everyone else does,' Elsie said, as if it were his business and not Bunny's at all. '*I* grew up in downtown Chatham –'

'Where's that?' Erica said.

'Kent, but you won't have missed anything by not knowing,' Elsie said. 'There were no marrows there. I didn't even know what colour green was till I went to school, but there was a blade of grass down by the station. We used to get taken on school trips to look at it. Every summer we'd book a coach and afterwards we'd all go back to school and do a project on grass. Then one year some idiot picked it to stick in his project folder, *but even I,*' Elsie yelled, '*know how to write on a marrow!*'

'I suppose you went to evening classes,' Bunny said. 'Look here, Else, that's not the carb or the fuel bowl.'

'Pity, they're easy,' Elsie said.

'I've won!' said Erica. 'You said if that wasn't the carb I'd get my money back.'

'We said if it was the exhaust,' Elsie corrected her. 'It might not be. Give the jets a blast with the air line.'

96

'If that is the exhaust,' Erica said, 'can I clean it? I'd rather do that than have the 3p.'

'I'd pay you threepence to do it,' Elsie said generously. 'O K, if it's the exhaust port you can clean it – but no prodding. I don't want all the muck to end up in the cylinder.'

'I know that,' Erica said. 'Now, how do you write on a marrow?'

'Ah,' said Elsie, 'you take your marrow when it is young and green, about six inches long –'

'That's a courgette,' Bunny said.

'Great oaks from little acorns grow.'

'Yes, but not from courgettes.'

'Little courgettes grow into big marrows. Now, find your tender young marrow, take a pin and inscribe on the surface anything you like; Kilroy was here, or Kilroy was somewhere else and he can prove it, and then let nature take its course . . .'

'What d'you mean?' Erica said. 'Look, that's not the jets, either. That *must* be the exhaust port.'

'All right, all right, you can take over. Get the exhaust pipe off – clamp first . . . What I mean is, you ignorant toads, that as the marrow gets bigger, the skin splits where the pin went in and the letters get bigger too. It can look very artistic if you've got decent handwriting, although Times Roman is best if you have to print.'

'Auntie Joan'll put on her parts if I start writing on her marrows,' Erica said.

'Putting on her parts? What kind of talk is that?' Elsie said.

'Blowing up,' Erica said.

'Going spare,' said Elsie. 'Your Auntie Joan seems to be spare for much of the time; no mean feat for a lady of her dimensions. You must expect to suffer for your art. I once wrote a whole poem on a marrow and sent it to the Harvest Festival at school.'

'Get away,' Bunny said. 'What did they harvest at your school – iron filings?'

'Car batteries, mostly,' Elsie said, 'but somebody shopped the fence.'

'What was the poem?' Bunny asked. 'Look, isn't it time one of us had a look at Freddie's Honda? We can't put that off for ever and the insurance bloke'll be in soon.'

'Which one is it?'

'Norwich Union.'

'He's fast. Bring it in then,' Elsie said.

'You'll have to help. I can't wheel that. You know where the forks are.'

'What was the marrow poem?' Erica asked. The exhaust pipe lifted away from its mounting. 'Yuk! Look at that. I *told* you.'

'I know, I know. Now, take off the cylinder head, move the piston down to BDC...'

'I know, I know...'

'Then you can prod all you like. Use a screwdriver.' Elsie stood up and declaimed:

> *'Mr Smith is long and narrow,*
> *Mrs Smith is like this marrow.*
> *The skin is hard and so's the pith.*
> *The same is true of Mrs Smith.*

The headmaster went out of his mind but he never discovered who'd done it.'

'Who was Mrs Smith?' Erica asked.

'His wife,' Elsie said. 'She taught the infants. Oh, that poem didn't do her justice. She wasn't like a marrow, she was like a conference pear; rough, mottled and bottom-heavy. A bad case of Duck's Disease, that lady, but she inspired me to write my poem. Not bad for eleven.'

'You haven't changed much in twenty years,' Bunny observed sourly, dragging Freddie's injured Honda towards the hoist.

Elsie went to help him mount it and Erica bent over the clogged exhaust port, trying to think of something she could

98

write on a marrow, and at the same time seeing a boy just like Elsie, smaller but with the same scrambled hair, crouching in a marrow patch with a pin; but it was a cloudy picture. She found it very hard to imagine Elsie as a boy, but it was even harder to imagine Mum, say, or Auntie Joan as little girls, although she had seen them in photographs. And it was more difficult still to envisage herself over thirty, like Elsie. She had always supposed that anyone over thirty had one foot in the grave, or at least a couple of toes, but Elsie didn't really seem to be any age at all. It seemed likely that his tale of Mrs Smith and the marrows had been all lies, and he had always been just as he was now.

'I bet,' Elsie said, suddenly, behind her, 'I bet you can't make orange-peel teeth, either. Oh, the rural crafts of old England are dying fast.'

Chapter Twelve

'Swedes don't sell,' Erica said, next morning. 'Marrows are all right – people always think they're getting a bargain when they buy a marrow. We didn't sell *any* swedes, yesterday. Carrots'd be better.'

'Well, set out the stall and see what're left,' Auntie Joan said, grudgingly. She stared at the sky. 'I don't reckon we'll get many customers today. That look a bit greasy on towards Norwich. We'll have rain before lunchtime.'

Erica went out into the garden. Robert followed her closely.

'Don't you go taking nothing my mum said you wasn't to take,' he cautioned her.

'She didn't say I *couldn't* take anything,' Erica said. 'That was what I *don't* want to take we were arguing about. Go on, then. What did she say I couldn't take, then? Eh?'

She was desperate for Robert to go away. In her pocket, stuck through several layers of denim, was a wicked long pin from Auntie Joan's sewing box. It had a blue glass head and was probably an antique, a fit instrument with which to write on marrows. If only Robert would take himself off; he would have several fits, if not forty, put on his parts, go spare –

however that was done – like Mr Smith the headmaster, if he caught her even handling one. In the end she managed to lose him round by the greenhouse, and made off for the marrow patch. She recalled Elsie's advice about choosing the right marrow; the one hanging from the Bramley looked just the right size, but if she wrote on that someone would be sure to spot it, and there would certainly be parts put on. It would be safer to find one of the outlying marrows that were ripening shadily in the long grass under the great thorny leathery leaves, and there were plenty of these. Erica fought her way through the barbs and tendrils and found three likely candidates growing at intervals on one stem. The largest was no longer than her hand and she was afraid that she would have to go back to Norwich before they grew big enough to be legible. Elsie must have had very neat handwriting to have got a whole poem onto such a small surface.

She took out her pin and on the first marrow wrote MERCURY MOTOR CYCLES, on the second, ERICA TIMPERLEY WAS HERE and on the third, ELSIE WAINWRIGHT RULES OK, thinking that perhaps she would give it to him as a present. It was much harder than she had expected. The pin went through the skin easily, too easily, and even when she had finished it was very difficult to see what she had written. In any case, she had no idea of what the inscriptions would look like, having only Elsie's word for it that they would look like anything at all, but as she was finishing RULES OK on the third marrow she noticed that the writing on the first was beginning to show dark green against the paler skin. Encouraged, she added a flourishing question mark after OK on Elsie's marrow, and drew some bold scrolls and curlicues underneath. By this time the first marrow was looking distinctly decorative; it seemed a pity to stop now, just as she was finding out how well she could do it.

She tracked two more vines into the undergrowth, selected her marrows and wrote, VOTE LABOUR, BAN THE BOMB, ROBERT IS A FAT TWIT and COME TO SUNNY CALSTEAD

101

FOR YOUR HOLIDAY. She also decorated one marrow in fish scales, with a wide eye in the middle. It looked very sinister and she covered it up.

BAN THE BOMB could go back to Norwich with her, for Mr Pearson next door, who would approve, and VOTE LABOUR might come in handy for the next election, if it lasted that long, but as she was drawing a beaming sun alongside COME TO SUNNY CALSTEAD Calstead ceased to be sunny and it began to rain. Erica plunged the pin back into her pocket and into her leg, backed out of the bushes and ran to the house with the trug full of vegetables.

'Now where have you been?' Auntie Joan demanded. 'I've been down to Beth Nudd's and back while you've been out.' She looked hard at Erica's mouth. 'Have you been at the red currants?'

'I never.' Erica had no cover story ready. She thought furiously. 'I was getting the ducks out of the peas.'

It was the right answer. 'Ducks? How many? What sort of ducks?'

'About six – I couldn't count. They kept moving about. Those little brown spotty ones.'

'Mallards,' Robert said, with hatred. He was hunched over a cat's cradle of wire and skewers anchored with Plasticine to a square of chipboard. It looked like a model of a radio telescope, but was probably a slug trap. 'They're the worst, them old mallards are. They bite you with their hard beaks.'

'They don't.' Erica often fed the ducks at home on the Wensum, where it ran under Fye Bridge. As soon as one piece of bread hit the water glad cries could be heard in either direction and whole flotillas of ducks, each trailing a V-shaped wake, would converge. 'They just suck you a bit if you don't feed them fast enough. Their beaks are all soft inside.'

'Well, you can't go to Polthorpe in this rain. Go and put Cellophane over the stall.'

'I've got to. They're expecting me. We've got the table there, and everything.'

'See if that stop later. You can't take the bicycle out in the rain. That'll rust.'

Rubbish, Erica said to herself, as she went out to cover the stall with Cellophane. In fact it was polythene, but apparently the word had not yet reached Calstead. The rain was soft and persistent, like somebody nagging and trying to be nice about it. It was the kind of rain that seemed not to settle, until you touched your coat or hair and found that it had soaked right through to the skin, but the Iron Cow was so covered in black paint, even to the wheel rims, that there was scarcely anything to rust except for the crumpled horns, which were rusty in any case; and Erica had seen an old oilskin cape hanging up in the garage. She went in and unhooked it, to try it on. It reached to the ground and made her feel like a huge inverted marrow flower, especially when she put on the yellow sou'wester that went with it. Creaking like a tree in a high wind, she went back to the house.

Robert pretended to be speechless with mirth. He ogled and pointed, tipping his chair so far back that Erica had reasonable grounds for hoping that it would slide from under him and dump him on the back of his neck.

Auntie Joan looked at her. 'That belonged to your grandad,' she said. 'He wore that when he went out on his tricycle.'

'That'll keep me dry,' Erica said. 'And the bike, and the vegetables. That'll cover everything.'

It did indeed cover everything. Riding past Mrs Nudd's shop at the corner, Erica risked a sidelong glance and saw that the skirts of the oilskin cleared the ground by only a few centimetres, concealing all of Erica and most of the Iron Cow from below the wheel hubs. There was something indefinably sinister about the yellow shape gliding silently through Mrs Nudd's two dark plateglass windows with no visible means of locomotion. Even her hands were out of sight beneath the oilskin and when she rang the rusty bell a muffled grinding sound filled the yellow tent.

As she turned into the doorway of the Cave Elsie dropped an entire socket set on the floor (an accident that was probably totally unconnected with her arrival) and cried, 'Good grief, it's the Dreaded Yellow Jelly Mould, come to get us.'

'I can't get off!' Erica shrieked, wobbling perilously round the Indian. Bunny sprang up from the floor, where he was picking small particles of Eastern Counties Omnibus from the remains of Freddie's Honda, and caught her. Elsie took the oilskin by the shoulders and supported it while Erica slid out from underneath and off the Iron Cow, all in one movement. The oilskin was so stiff that it stood up on its own, with the sou'wester balanced over the neck hole. Bunny wheeled the whole ensemble into a corner where it crouched malevolently, waiting for her to come back and bring it to life again.

Elsie had brought the table indoors and already yesterday's unsold vegetables, all the swedes and one forlorn marrow, were lying on it.

'I hope you brought some friends to keep them company,' Elsie said. 'Freddie's missus bought the other marrow.'

'That's carrots and beetroots and things like that, today,' Erica said. 'Things that people really want. You won't have to bribe them, this time.'

'Bribe?' said Bunny. 'That was demanding with menaces, if you ask me.'

'We didn't ask you,' Elsie said.

Erica was wondering if she were destined to be the Dreaded Yellow Jelly Mould for ever more in Elsie's kingdom, and if this really were the handle that she wanted. It would have to be shortened, surely. Was Jelly any better, or Mouldy? It was almost as bad as being called Yob.

'I've got just the job for you,' Elsie said, as she laid out the vegetables. 'Something that needs a thin hand.'

'I haven't got a thin hand.'

'Aw, c'mon now,' Elsie wheedled. 'You must have *one*; *somewhere*. Thinner than mine, anyhow.' His hands were square and crosshatched with oil, as you would expect to see on a mechanic. Erica remembered that she had meant to look at his handwriting on an invoice. It was likely that that, too, would be black and square, but he had once written a whole poem on a baby marrow.

'It's not so much a thin hand we need as a thin wrist. Tappet clearance,' Elsie said, and introduced Erica to the machine she was to work on. Its owner stood by it with a cup of coffee.

'Yerbut,' Elsie said, by way of introduction.

'I'm ... the Dreaded Yellow Jelly Mould,' Erica said, uncertainly.

'Eh?' Yerbut said. He did not say, 'Yer, but ...'

'This is Erica,' Elsie said, so she still had no handle. 'Your mechanic for today.'

'Yer, but ...' said Yerbut.

'Yer but nothing,' Elsie said, firmly. 'She knows what she's about.'

'Yer, but suppose she mucks that up. Suppose you brought a television set in and I gave that to the Gremlin to mend. What would you say then?'

'I'd say you were out of your tree, and I'd be right,' Elsie said. 'However, Erica will do a proper job, or I'll nobble her marrows,' he added over his shoulder to Erica, 'and anyway, I can't, offhand, think of any television set worth even approximately as little as your Suzuki. Which reminds me, isn't it time the works wireless came back?'

'Yer, but that needs *parts*,' said Yerbut.

'Whaddya mean, parts?' said Elsie. 'It's got a circuit board in it, hasn't it?'

'No that hent,' Yerbut said. 'That's got *valves*. Gawd struth, Elsie, when did you last have the back off?'

'Not since I was at university,' Elsie admitted. Ten years ago, Erica thought, bending to the Suzuki. 'Anyway, I don't understand electronics. I never pretended I did,' he went on, self-righteously. 'If I did, I wouldn't have given it to you to mend, would I? I'd have done it myself.'

'Yer, but that hent electronics,' Yerbut said. 'That hent

105

got anything to do with electricity at all, if you ask me. You'd get better reception if you plugged that into the gas main.'

'Well, you said it was gas state,' Elsie said, smirking.

'Like your head,' said Yerbut. He glared down at Erica. 'His life,' he said, pointing to Elsie, 'is in your hands. You muck up my bike and bits of Elsie will be stopping the draught under my door. I'll *unravel* him,' Yerbut said, as he went out.

'Where were you at college?' Erica said.

'UEA,' Elsie said. 'That's how I came to know Norfolk and love it – enough to know that it was better than Chatham, at any rate.'

'University? For being a mechanic?'

'No, for being a nutter,' Bunny said, from his communion with Freddie's Honda. 'He didn't get a degree – he was certified.'

'I have a degree,' Elsie said, loftily. 'But I'm not going to tell you what it is; you'll only laugh.'

'A degree of sarcasm,' Bunny muttered. 'You didn't do a lot with it though, did you?'

'I taught for a year,' Elsie said, unexpectedly. 'It was horrible. The school was so enormous that the headmaster didn't even know the teachers' names, let alone the kids'.'

'Pull the other one.'

'Straight up. He never knew mine, for a start. I decided to get out when he mistook me for one of his prefects and bawled me out for smoking in the bus queue. As I walked away swearing – I'd probably have got the stick if he'd heard me – I passed a motor-cycle dealer at the end of the road. They had a Gold Flash in the window –'

'Like on the sign?' Erica said.

'The model for it. So I thought, what the hell and went in and bought it. It was in shocking condition, but I did it up and sold it. Which was just as well, as I'd only that day handed in my resignation. I went along to the headmaster's room and put up my hand. "Please, sir, I want to go home." He told me to make an appointment if I wanted to see him.

He said, "Sixth-formers have to obey the rules too, Durrant."
I said, "I'm not Durrant, I'm Wainwright." He said, "I don't
care who you are, make an appointment," and then I remembered that Durrant was the cross-eyed creep who ran the
debating club. He had ten O-levels. I hated him. Anyway,
I made my appointment and resigned. He said, "I think you're
making a wise decision, McCrae." '

'Batten down hatches,' Bunny said. 'Gremlin sighted on
starboard bow and Gremlin's mother right behind.'

'They must be having a slack time at the chippy,' Elsie
said, glumly. He went and stood in the doorway, where the
Gremlin and Mrs Kermit were approaching. Already the yard
was puddled with murky water and the rain made pockmarks
in the puddles. Mrs Kermit, in a mauve nylon overall and
carrying a frog-green umbrella, stepped round them; the
Gremlin charged straight through in showers of gritty spray,
with his prodding stick at the ready. Elsie fielded him, turned
him round, and sent him back the way he had come, with
the smoothness of long practice.

'Oh Elsie,' Mrs Kermit said, furling her umbrella point-
foremost, so that she looked as if she too were going a-
prodding. 'John just rang up from Wroxham. The bike have
broke down and he want to know if you can go and pick
that up.'

'What, now?' Elsie said.

'Or pick him up,' Mrs Kermit said, very agitated. The
ferrule of the umbrella was pointing dangerously at Elsie's
left nostril. 'He just missed the eleven forty and he've got to
be back here to take out the twelve twenty. He's afraid he'll
be late if he start walking and try to hitch.'

'I've got a bone in my leg.' Elsie limped a few paces, un-
convincingly. 'And a lot on, right now.' *That's* a whopper,
Erica thought. 'Can't you go?'

'But the car won't start in the rain,' Mrs Kermit wailed,
and the umbrella jigged frantically. Elsie closed his hand over
his nose. 'And we had to take the front seat out to get the

angle-irons in. I mean, that's still full of iron. What'd I do with Gordon?'

'Put him in the boot?' Bunny mumbled in the background.

Erica began to understand that Gordon was the Gremlin and that John must be Kermit and that Kermit was a bus driver. Perhaps it was Kermit's bus that Freddie had ridden into; it was an increasingly small world.

'I suppose I couldn't leave Gordon here? Alan won't have him in the shop on his own.'

'You amaze me,' Elsie said, reaching out again to turn the Gremlin as he charged.

'That is, if the car'll start . . .'

The Gremlin attached himself to Elsie with the enthusiasm of a young vampire bat. Elsie jumped and swore horribly. There was a shocked silence.

'Control yourself,' Bunny reproved him severely. 'Ladies present.'

Mrs Kermit blushed, but not at Elsie's outburst. 'Did he bite you? Oh, Gordon, we don't bite people do we, pet. That's not nice.' She looked at the ring of small indentations on Elsie's wrist. 'Bite him back.'

'No, no,' Elsie said, hurriedly. 'Don't worry about it. I'll go – before the rabies sets in. Where's he waiting?'

'He said he'd be in the bus shelter by the car park,' Mrs Kermit cried, and turned to bob away again through the puddles, the umbrella floating in the wind above her head like a water-lily leaf in a strong current. Elsie came back into the cave, square-jawed and stern.

'Right, you people,' he said, out of the corner of his mouth, 'the success of this operation depends on your pulling together. I'm relying on you to see this thing through.'

'What thing?' Bunny said, crossly. 'Do talk straight for once, Else.' Erica knew better and leaped to attention with a salute that made her elbow crack.

'I'm depending on *you*,' Elsie said, 'and *him*,' pointing to Bunny, 'to back me up, especially as I'm only doing it to keep that little monster out of my workshop. I myself am boldly going where no man has gone before. Wroxham, the final frontier ...'

'Do give it a rest,' Bunny pleaded. 'You're out half the time, anyway.'

'No moral fibre,' Elsie said, sadly. 'I may be some time,' he continued, through gritted teeth. 'Carry on, chaps.' He dived away across the soupy ground and scrambled into the driving seat of the dreadful old Ford Zephyr that Erica had taken for a wreck, although now, as Elsie turned it in a differential-wrenching circle, she saw that behind it was a trailer hooked on to a shiny new tow ball.

'He's going to lose that one day,' Bunny remarked, gloomily. 'He'll go one way and the trailer'll go the other. I think he's out to lunch, sometimes. He's right about us keeping the show going, though. D'you make a decent cup of tea, Erica?'

Erica, not failing to notice that Bunny included her among the people who kept Elsie's business ticking over, made one last bid for her handle.

'I'm the Dreaded Yellow Jelly Mould,' she said.

'If you are,' Bunny advised her, 'I shouldn't advertise the fact.' He crouched, a melancholy hulk, behind the Indian, the bones of his T-shirt showing at the neck of his boilersuit. 'Just put the kettle on, there's a good girl.'

Chapter Thirteen

The telephone rang while Erica was in the cupboard by the filing cabinet, filling the kettle. Bunny rose massively to answer it and nodded into the receiver as if it were telling him bad news that he'd been expecting. When Erica came back he put the handset down and scribbled on a pad.

'That's another message for old Arrow,' he said. 'Run across with that, will you?'

'Who's old Arrow? *Where* is he?' She pushed the plug into the kettle, gave it the quarter turn recommended by Elsie and stood well back to switch on at the wall, in the approved house style, with an insulated screwdriver.

'He's the plumber,' Bunny said. 'Very popular fellow, cheap, fast and reliable, but he's moonlighting. No one's supposed to know, so he works from the back – over next-door-but-one to the dentist.'

'What's he moonlighting from?' Erica asked, wiping her hands on the cleanest of the oily rags.

'The dole,' Bunny said, 'so keep your mouth shut. Strictly speaking, I suppose, he's a cowboy, but that's good quality cow. He hasn't got a phone so we take his messages for him.

That's how I know he's so popular.' The telephone rang again and Bunny reached for it, holding out the note in his other hand. 'See what I mean?'

'That might be for Elsie.'

'Chance'd be a fine thing.'

Erica took the note as Bunny edged back into the booth. The rain was coming down harder now, like a child's drawing of rain, thick dark lines of it all leaning in one direction. It would be too arduous to climb into the oilskin, and if she were not to be the Dreaded Yellow Jelly Mould it was pointless anyway. She took the sou'wester, poked the message under it for safety and dry-keeping, and went out into the weather.

She had hardly expected to find a dentist practising on an industrial estate, even on one of this size. Perhaps he used a block and tackle for extracting teeth, and concrete for fillings, and a pneumatic drill; but when she reached the corner where Bunny had directed her she found that it was only the same dentist whose brass plate she had seen in the Street. His surgery was built out at the back, and through the window she saw a lighted room with elegant menacing gantries and lamps, and cabinets full of things, as on Elsie's shelves only, presumably, tooth-sized.

Next door was a decrepit shed with *Rat's Castle* scrawled on the door, and Arrow's establishment was next to that; just a normal back door, painted green. What once must have been Arrow's back garden had become part of the industrial estate, for she could see the remains of a cinder path with black barley-sugar edging, and there were still one or two discouraged plants huddled up under the window-sill. She knocked and waited, wishing that Arrow had a porch and wiping the rain from her glasses. There were furtive sounds inside, and at last the door opened.

'Yes?'

Erica took the message from under her sou'wester. 'Mr Arrow?'

'Bowen,' said the man, who was not so very old after all.

III

Erica looked at the note. *Mr Bowen*, Bunny had written on it. She handed it over.

'Thank you,' said Mr Bowen. He still did not sound pleased.

'I'm sorry,' Erica said. 'I thought Bunny said that was for Mr Arrow.'

'Very likely,' said the man, 'but that's Bowen. Thank you,' he said. 'That bloody Elsie and his bloody silly names,' he added as he shut the door.

Erica sprinted back across the yard. Halfway over she stopped.

Bowen. Arrow. She could not have misheard. Bowen did not sound a bit like Arrow.

Bowen. Arrow. Bowen Arrow, Bowen . . . bow and arrow . . .

Obviously some handles were not for public use. She felt that she had put her foot in it.

When she reached home there was a letter from Mum awaiting her. It was on the dresser, propped against a china jug, and Robert, propped against the dresser, was looking at it. Erica felt that being looked at by Robert could not do the letter any good, and picked it up.

'What's that say?' Robert demanded. 'Who've sent that? Who'd write to *you*?'

'That's from my mum,' Erica said. 'Who writes to *you*?'

'What've she got to say?' Auntie Joan asked. Erica, slightly surprised and not very pleased by their interest, held the envelope by the extreme corner, considering how to get out of opening it while they were watching. She was remembering all the things that she had put in her own letter, and wondering how many of them Mum had replied to, and *how* she had replied. It might not be the kind of letter that ought to be opened in front of Auntie Joan. Robert was leaning towards her as though trying to read it through the envelope. (Fat chance, Erica thought. Fat chance he can read at all.)

'Well, open that then,' Auntie Joan was saying. It only

needed Uncle Peter to walk in and she would have a full house.

'Not till I've washed,' Erica cried, with sudden inspiration. 'Look – I'm all over oil.' She poked the letter down inside her T-shirt and flapped black greasy palms at them, turning towards the door and the staircase.

'You hent going to use the bathroom in that state,' Auntie Joan said; telling her, not asking her. The bathroom at Hall Farm Cottage was a place you went into only when you were clean enough not to make a mess of it by washing. Surface grime had to be taken off in the kitchen. Balked of privacy, Erica turned to the sink.

'I don't know what Anne'll say when you go home with those fingernails,' Auntie Joan remarked.

I know what she'd say if I went home without them, Erica thought.

'All oil, down to the quick!'

Auntie Joan turned on the hot water so that Erica would not have to sully the polished taps, which were treated to a quick buff with a dishcloth every time they were used, and handed her the block of rough green soap which always felt to Erica more like pumice stone than soap, until it got wet and went slimy. She took a long time washing her hands, soaping and sluicing, scrubbing at the offending nails and cuticles with the fierce brush that, until she had discovered Howlett's yard, only Uncle Peter had ever got dirty enough to use. She hoped very much that by the time she had finished – and she delayed that moment by carefully wiping out the bowl – they would have forgotten about the letter, but while she was drying off on the dank huckaback towel that hung behind the door Uncle Peter came in.

'Erica have had a letter,' Robert announced. Erica had not understood what receiving a letter at Hall Farm Cottage might involve. The first one from Mum had arrived while Auntie Joan was hoovering and Robert was in his bedroom, not making his bed. She had found it on the doormat when she came in from the garden and had opened it on the spot, in private, and in any case there had been nothing in it that called for concealment.

'That might be bad news,' Robert was saying hopefully. There was no escape. Erica took the letter out of her T-shirt, and stalled a little longer by tucking it under her arm while she wiped her glasses. No one moved. She took a paring knife from the draining-board and slid it under the flap ... there was an escape after all. The envelope contained a postcard with Craig's writing on it, all loops, like black cotton crochet. There was a letter too, but using the presence of the postcard as cover Erica screwed up the envelope, with the letter still in it, and shoved it into her pocket.

'That have got one of them new stamps on,' Robert said. 'Can I have that?'

'That's just an ordinary one,' Erica said, turning the back of the postcard towards him. On the front was a photograph of a green Yorkshire hill with white Yorkshire sheep grazing under a blue Yorkshire sky. It could have been anywhere – except Norfolk.

'No,' Robert persisted. 'On the envelope.'

'Let him have that, then,' Auntie Joan said protectively, as if Erica had refused. 'You don't collect them.'

Erica, on the point of inventing an enormous and comprehensive philatelic collection back home, had to extract the envelope and tear off the corner without revealing that there was a letter inside.

'That's First Class,' Uncle Peter remarked. 'Fancy wasting a First Class stamp to forward a postcard. Whyever didn't she just readdress that?'

'There's no room,' Erica said, exhibiting Craig's huge loopy handwriting.

'Second Class would have done,' Auntie Joan said. 'Are you sure there hent nothing else in the envelope?'

'That's empty,' Erica assured her, poking the envelope further into her pocket.

'I mean,' Auntie Joan said, 'Second Class would have got

114

here sooner or later. That hent hardly urgent, are it? Not a postcard.'

Craig had written, *There are a lot of hills here, and a lot of sheep.* Certainly it could not be passed off as urgent.

Erica improvised rapidly. 'Well ... Mum usually buys a lot of stamps at once. Perhaps she only had First Class ones left. I mean, she probably didn't want to have to go out specially for a Second Class one – not in this rain.'

'She'd have had to go out to post that,' Uncle Peter said.

'That may not be raining in Norwich,' Auntie Joan said.

Robert said, 'Oh, I've already got this one,' and threw the controversial stamp into the sink tidy.

Erica went upstairs to uncrease her letter and read it in peace, grinding her teeth, the teeth she had lied through, and knowing that she was going to have to lie through them again.

She sat on the bed and ironed the letter over her knee, but the paper was thin and porous and Mum's tiny hand-writing seemed to have been soaked up in the crankles. She had to hold it at various angles against the light before she could read it all, tilting it this way and that like a maze puzzle with rolling silver balls, and what she found was not reassuring.

Dear Erica, it said, *that dont look as if youre having a very good time does it?* Mum did not go in for apostrophes, unless they had all leaked away into the grooves of the paper. *Dadll be out North Walsham way on Saturday and he can come over and pick you up, you had better think of a good excuse for Joan or do you want me to write, thats a pity she hasnt got a phone.*

Some full stops seemed to have got out as well. Too right that's a pity, Erica thought, reading it again. *You can tell Joan hell . . .*

Hell? Erica thought. I wouldn't dare. Oh, *he'll . . .*

. . . be by at about half-past four Ill send a note shall I?

Erica looked at the top of the paper. The address was there, but no date. Today was Wednesday; the letter had probably been posted on Tuesday, or Monday night, and by now

Mum's note to Auntie Joan might well be on its way after it. She sat on the bed and cursed, thinking about that other Wednesday, only a week ago incredibly, when she had broken the television, quarrelled with Robert and written to Mum. It was also the day that she had discovered Elsie and his kingdom, but she had been in a filthy temper when she wrote that letter, sitting up in bed, and it had never occurred to her that Mum would do anything about fetching her home early; she had simply wanted to make sure that Mum knew how much she was suffering. She tried to remember whether or not she had mentioned Elsie in the letter. Probably not: it had been all veiled hints about Robert; especially the part written after the television debacle and the advent of the green shape.

The only thing to do was to nip out at once, down to the telephone box at Calstead Corner, and ring home. Erica stared out over the garden. The rain was now coming down so hard that it looked like a second sheet of wet and misty glass beyond the window, obscuring everything but the nearest rows of sugar beet on the far side of the dyke. Auntie Joan would be calling her down for tea at any moment now, and the rain was not likely to have stopped by the time they had finished eating. There was no chance that she could slip out unnoticed. Auntie Joan would be sure to ask where she was going, and then want to know why; if Erica told the truth, she would be suspicious about the letter, and if Erica lied, saying that she simply wanted to go for a walk, Auntie Joan would tell her not to. Erica could hardly blame her for that. Only a frog or a lunatic would want to go for a walk in this weather. She leaned on the window-sill and rehearsed various untruths.

'I just remembered – I had to ring my mate ...'

'I've got a bit of a headache and I wanted some fresh air ...' No, there were things in bottles in the bathroom for headaches.

'I think I dropped something down by the shop on my way home ...' What, a clanger?

'I just thought that Mum might have meant to put a letter

116

in the envelope and left that out by mistake so I thought I'd better ring up and find out.' Brilliant.

'You can't go out in this,' Auntie Joan would say.

'But that might be urgent. She wouldn't have written otherwise. She *hates* writing letters.' Even more brilliant, and true. She went downstairs.

'Go out?' said Auntie Joan. 'Well, no, you can't. Not in this.'

Erica riffled frantically through her lies. Now that she was standing in front of Auntie Joan she could see only too well that none of them would do.

'I just wanted to go for a walk,' Erica said. 'I could wear the Dreaded Yellow – the oilskin.'

'No.'

'Just down to the corner. I thought I could ring Mum.'

'Ring Anne?' Auntie Joan said. 'Whatever for?'

Let's give that a whirl, Erica thought. 'Well, I thought she might have meant to put a letter in the envelope and forgot. I mean, that *was* a First Class stamp ...'

'Don't be so soft,' Auntie Joan said. 'If she've forgot that she'll have sent that, separate.'

'But that might be urgent.'

'If that's urgent, she'll have sent that on anyway, won't she?'

Erica went back upstairs again. If only Auntie Joan had a telephone; but then, she thought, it would be impossible to make a call without the whole family listening in; not accidentally and secretively as people did at home when the door was not quite shut, but all lined up round the set as if they were listening to the radio. There was only one way out, as far as she could see, and that was to waylay the postman when he called in the morning, and if Mum's letter to Auntie Joan did not arrive by first post, to come home early from Polthorpe and catch him second time round in the afternoon. One way or another, that letter had to disappear. Then, while she was in Polthorpe, she could stop at a phone box and ring home to tell Mum that on no account did she want Dad to come and collect her on Saturday afternoon. It would be miserable to leave Calstead and the access to Elsie's kingdom before she needed to, but how much worse it would feel to be hauled off home when she no longer wanted to go; such a waste!

Chapter Fourteen

But it was so wet in the morning that there was no question of going out to hijack the mail. It was so wet that Auntie Joan did not even ask Erica to go out and collect the vegetables, as there was no point in setting up the stall.

'And you hent going to Polthorpe,' Auntie Joan said, before Erica had even spoken of going.

They had met on the landing, Auntie Joan carrying armfuls of clean sheets. Erica dodged back into her room and threw herself on the bed. If she could not go to Polthorpe she could not telephone, in which case it would not matter whether or not the letter arrived.

Yes, it would. Auntie Joan would still wonder what had been going on. There would be explanations called for. Then she recalled that on more than one occasion Auntie Joan had handed letters to the postman, instead of walking down to the post office. If Erica could only get a letter written in the next five minutes, and creep out to meet the post, she might smuggle a message out that way. She began to feel like a secret agent as she searched her carrier bags for the note pad and envelopes that she had brought with her ... and stamps ...

she must have a stamp ... *surely*. Luck was with her at last; she had a stamp; now for the letter.

Dear Mum, its all right now, I dont want to come home as things have got much more interesting since I wrote ... She left out *her* apostrophes, too, in case Mum thought that she was showing off.

It was Auntie Joan's day for changing the bed linen. Erica knew that she ought to go and help, and that she was expected to, but she stayed downstairs in the scullery doorway, watching the road across the gravel patch through the window. With the rain upsetting the day's routine there was no telling where anyone was supposed to be at any given moment. If the mail van drew up and there was only the one letter delivered, Auntie Joan might be by the back bedroom window at just the moment when she would find out about it and demand to know where it had got to; in which case Erica would either have to hand it over or pretend that it had been for her, which would mean hurriedly concealing the evidence and inventing the contents. Worse still, Robert might see it and come galloping out to grab the mail; she had no idea where he was and the van was already late, no doubt delayed by the rain.

Erica stood poised, one ear on Auntie Joan thumping about upstairs, one on the road, tuned to the sound of the mail van, and wished desperately for a third ear to keep open for Robert. She began to wonder where you would wear a third ear if you had one. On the forehead, possibly, like a bracket fungus, or perhaps it would not resemble an ear at all, but look more like a radio antenna on top of the head, which would be useful because you could then rotate it and pick up signals.

Her left ear picked up sounds of Robert in the living-room, at the same time as the right ear detected the mail van halting in the road outside. As usual the postman leaped out almost before the brakes were applied, and simultaneously Erica leaped out too, across the scullery, flinging open the back door as she landed on the mat and holding out her letter to the postman.

To her relief he took it and handed her three in return. Erica had scanned them thoroughly before she stepped inside again. The one with Mum's small handwriting on it was the smallest and she had it folded and shoved up her sleeve before Robert came up behind her and whipped the other two out of her hands.

He stomped upstairs to give them to his mother and Erica tiptoed behind him, heart walloping and head bent to hide her flushed face. It was, she knew, a terrible thing to interfere with Her Majesty's Mails, but all the same she went into the bathroom, locked the door and, without reading it, tore the letter into very small pieces and flushed them down the loo.

'Go out?' said Auntie Joan. 'Well, no, you can't. Not in this.'

'But they're expecting me. I've not been for two days.'

'Oh, nonsense. They don't actually want you there, do they?'

'Yes they do. I help with the bikes.'

'Help with the bikes?' This was not Auntie Joan's idea of a nice occupation for a young girl. 'I don't know what Anne would say.'

Erica knew that Mum would not mind one way or the other, so long as Erica had something to do. If Auntie Joan knew what Erica got up to in the evenings in Norwich she would never say such a fond thing.

'That yard,' said Auntie Joan, meaning Howlett's Industrial Estate, 'that'll be like a swamp by now, let alone the drains.'

Erica knew about the drains, although it was not the drains themselves that were the problem so much as what they drained. Howlett's, in a rare burst of public spirit, by Elsie's account, had provided two lavatories for the yard, and the drainage was eccentric. Bunny had mentioned the drains, fretfully, on Wednesday afternoon. Even then, after only half a day's rain, Elsie had put up a board across the doorway and laid a plank over the deepest puddle. It was now Saturday, and, apart from a slight dry interval on the previous night when the sudden moonlight had surprised Erica from sleep, the rain had not stopped falling. Erica looked out of the kitchen window over the garden, where it was now too wet even to go and search for vegetables. At least the marrows would be fattening, their skins splitting along the lines of her graffiti, but so would everything else. Erica grimly imagined the swollen pods and waterlogged roots that were waiting to be collected when at last the clouds moved on, but they were now moving out to sea in deep wallowing troughs and ridges, like wet blankets in a washing machine, and as they went another lot piled up behind them. Somewhere in the fields the peacock wailed.

This time last week, she thought, glaring under the curtain and through the steamy pane, she had been afraid to go back to Elsie's kingdom in case he were tired of her. Now she was afraid that if she did not go back soon, he would forget who she was. The vegetables on the stall would wither into a little compost heap and Elsie would look at them and wonder how they came to be there. She was only a name. She had no handle.

The rain went on and on. In the afternoon Auntie Joan put on a coat and boots and stumped off across the fields to clean the church before tomorrow's service and to arrange the flowers. Erica offered to come and help, but Auntie Joan seemed to have decided that Erica must be kept dry at all costs, like something that might dissolve, and told her to stay behind.

She sat at the table in the living-room, on a hard upright chair behind the settee where Uncle Peter and Robert sat watching sport on the television. She could easily have sat at ease in one of the armchairs and shared their salted peanuts, but she felt that if she were going to be angry she might as well do it in proper discomfort. In any case, they would scarcely notice whether she were there or not; their eyes never left the screen. It was as if they were watching something holy, a vision of angels that would fade if they took their eyes off it, while a voice yammered over all, 'Oh, look at *that*. Just look at *that*! *Look* at that! Oooooh ...'

What could you do *but* look at it, Erica thought.

Six athletes with pale citrus legs cantered across the screen and rounded the corner of their track towards Erica's green shape. During the week it had grown smaller but more concentrated, like the spot behind your eyelids after you have looked at the sun.

'Can't see a thing no more,' Robert complained.

'Elbows! Elbows! Oh, very rough!' the commentator cried madly. Evidently he could see something that they could not. Erica lifted the curtain again and squinted out. The rain seemed to have slackened very slightly; she could see individual drops, and the latest ridge of cloud was moving heavily but purposefully away from the house towards the coast.

She rose quietly and edged out of the room. Neither Robert nor Uncle Peter noticed; something exciting was happening on the screen. Maybe one of the runners had fallen over, or met with some more interesting mishap, for as she pulled the door to a voice shrieked, 'Oh, no, look at that, Brian. He is *literally* running on one leg ...'

The Yellow Jelly Mould was hanging where she had left it in the garage, and the Iron Cow stood against the wall, ready to be mounted. Erica put on the oilskin and wheeled the bicycle out into the rain. She had been wrong. It was not easing off, and an angry wind was now following the clouds, but already the oilskin streamed with water and questions might be asked if she hung it up again. If questions were going to be asked, she felt, she might as well furnish some answers. She climbed aboard the Iron Cow, draped the oilskin front and back, and pedalled away from the house. In two minutes she knew that she should have worn boots. Her trainers were soaked through to the insoles, but her own boots were in the kitchen cupboard at Tasburgh Court. Robert's would have fitted her, but she would rather have had sodden socks and cold feet with white wrinkled toes and blue nails than wear Robert's boots.

123

Polthorpe Street lay deserted except for a few idiot foreigners off the boats who had paid for their holiday and were determined to get their money's worth. Marsh's forecourt was empty of cars, but Elsie's sign was swinging giddily in the wind. There she stopped. Across the mouth of the alley was a barrier of old saw horses, broken pallets and scrap iron, and a notice which, by its spotty appearance, had been painted in the rain and put out before it had dried. There was an arrow pointing off to the left, and underneath; FLOODING!!! PLEASE USE REAR ENTRANCE.

Erica was already down from the saddle, and climbing up to it again, under the oilskin, would admit too much water. She hurried round the corner, down Broad Street and onto the sooty pitted track that led to the estate. The twin ruts were two parallel canals and the Iron Cow, contrary as ever, aimed its wheels at the one on the right and refused to come out. By now she was wishing that she had stayed on board, for what had been potholes before were now ponds, and she was up to her ankles in the widest before she realized that it was also the deepest. Her foot turned on a stone at the bottom and down she went, with the Iron Cow on top. On the bank a little wet creature jumped up and down, crowing with pleasure at the entertainment. It was the Gremlin.

Erica picked herself up, and the Iron Cow. The oilskin was waterlogged, with as much liquid inside as out, accumulated in unexpected pockets and creases. Ignoring the Gremlin she squelched towards Elsie's Cave, lit up and welcoming in the corner.

She could see at once why the alleyway had been barred. Elsie's end of the yard had become a grimy lake and across it, balanced on old oil cans, ran a whole network of planks that met in the middle of the lake on an island of pallets. It was undoubtedly a necessary arrangement, but Erica had the feeling that it was rather more complex than it needed to be, and she suspected that Elsie had been amusing himself while performing a public service. She mounted the nearest plank and walked the Iron Cow through the floods towards the Cave's mouth, where the water was held at bay by a rampart of sandbags.

Elsie looked out of the cave. 'Welcome to Venice. "Once did she hold the gorgeous East in fee, and was the safeguard of the West ..."'

'Do wrap up,' Bunny begged from somewhere inside.

'Who got caught in Copernicus, then?' Elsie said. He put one foot at the end of the plank that ran up onto the sandbags, lifted the Iron Cow over the barrage and lowered it to the floor on his own side. Erica jumped down after it.

'Caught in Copernicus?'

'Flat out, by the looks of it,' Elsie said. 'Take off your whale-skin, do, and come and dry out.'

'I thought Copernicus was a person,' Erica said, sinking into the folds of the cape as Elsie lifted it away from her. Water streamed from unlikely places.

'If you stood in a river in this,' Elsie said, 'you might catch a few eels at least. Copernicus was an astronomer.'

'And now he's a crater,' Bunny said, 'according to Elsie. On the moon.'

'And at the end of the yard,' Elsie said. 'The pothole. It's exactly the same shape – amazing coincidence.'

'No that's not,' Bunny growled. 'That wasn't the same shape at all until he took a sledge hammer and altered it.'

'I altered it because it wasn't big enough,' said Elsie.

'Not big enough? That's a health hazard,' Bunny said. 'There's things breeding at the bottom, now.'

'I got on to Howlett's to fill it in, and they said it wasn't worth bothering about, so I made it worth bothering about.'

'They didn't fill that in, though, did they?' Bunny said, triumphantly. 'And now look at it. That pothole's caused more punctures ... People think we keep it there to drum up custom.'

'*Our* customers come down the alley,' Elsie said. 'Only we've had to block it off. A hole has opened up.'

125

'What d'you call it?' Erica said.

'Call it? The hole? A hole with a *name?*'

'That'll have a name by the end of the afternoon,' Bunny said. 'Stop giving him ideas. Quit mardling and put the kettle on – no, hang about. You'll short circuit in that state. I'll do it. You go and get dry.'

Erica became aware that the Cave was filled with a dull roaring, like the furnace room at school, and that it was unusually warm. On either side of the dismantled Indian stood a gas heater fired from butane canisters, a paraffin heater with its booster switched on and an ancient black oil stove with holes in the top that threw a rose window of light onto the ceiling. A layer of steam floated just above her head, fed by the kettle and by a mist that rose from the floor and all around.

'Just as a matter of interest,' Elsie said, pouring boiling water into mugs, 'why did you come?'

Erica felt cold. She should have stayed at home.

'I thought there might be some work – did say I'd come and I couldn't – not Thursday and Friday – Auntie wouldn't let me.'

'Oh, that's all right, then,' Elsie said. 'I thought you might have come storming through the floods for Peter's leads.'

'I'd forgotten about them,' Erica said, thawing again.

'I bet Peter hasn't.'

'Too bad,' Bunny said. 'I reckon Elsie forgot whose they were and flogged them. He sold his own torque wrench once, by mistake.'

Elsie was stirring the coffee with a screwdriver.

'Ware Gremlin!' he said, suddenly. 'The subaquatic prodder. I wonder if he floats face down?'

Along the planks came the Gremlin, bouncing springily in red rubber boots. Elsie and Bunny, each with one foot on the sandbags, stood and watched him.

'Move the plank,' Bunny said. 'I dare you.'

'Don't be cruel,' Elsie rebuked him. To the Gremlin he said, 'Why don't you jump off in the middle and see how deep it is?'

The Gremlin stood on Pallet Island and pointed at Erica. 'She fell off. I saw her.'

'Why don't you go and find a deep hole and fill it – head down?' Bunny asked him. The Gremlin drew his prodding stick from behind his back and flourished it.

'I'm coming,' he threatened, and cantered along the last of the planks that led to the sandbags, with the stick held out murderously before him so that Bunny and Elsie had to swivel out of the way to avoid being transfixed. He landed with a wet smack on the cold concrete.

'Now what do we do?' Elsie asked, hopelessly. 'He's in.'

'Throw him back, he's too small to keep,' Bunny said.

'He might chew his way back in through the sandbags,' Elsie said. 'A sort of rotary lamprey.'

Bunny turned to Erica. 'You're a woman. What do you do with children? You must have been a babysitter in your time.'

Erica had never been called a woman before. 'I've sat with Barry Pearson, but he really is a baby – anyway, he's nice,' she said, looking distastefully at the Gremlin, who having found his way in was trotting busily round the Cave, prodding. He prodded, in turn, the Indian, both gas fires, the telephone which fell from its shelf and hung by a thread, clicking, and the dodgy socket where they plugged the kettle in.

'Nice or not, if we don't do something sharpish he'll be past bothering about,' said Elsie, with unholy surmise. 'Can't you take him for a little walk, Erica? Look, it's stopped raining.'

Chapter Fifteen

Bunny went outside several times and stood in the lake, to *prove* that it had stopped raining. Erica pretended not to believe him now that she knew what they were after.

'You wouldn't even need your Jelly Mould,' Elsie wheedled. He cornered the Gremlin and began to unpick his hand, finger by finger, from the handle of the stick. As he did so the other hand, grey and prehensile, closed round it. 'You are a horrible child,' Elsie said. 'You ought to be pickled in a jar. You ought to be put in slices under a microscope.' He applied himself to the second hand. 'Why don't you go and tell your mum that Elsie is a savage brute and not to be trusted with any child under the age of – how old are you, Erica?'

'Eleven.'

'Under the age of eleven.' The first hand was back in place. 'Erica,' Elsie pleaded, 'take him away. I'll pay you.'

'I'd rather help Bunny with the Indian.'

'So would I. I'd rather lie down in the road and let buses run over me, personally,' Elsie said. 'I know how you feel.'

'I can't go out in my trainers again,' Erica said. 'They're *soaked*. I was going to take them off and dry them.'

'Then you could paddle – with the Creature from the Black Lagoon,' Elsie said.

'Here we go,' Bunny moaned, resignedly. 'It was a puddle just now. Black Lagoon . . .'

'I've got some boots that might fit you,' Elsie said. 'In the office, under the shelf. Have a look.'

The office was the glass booth where the telephone lived. Erica picked up the telephone and replaced it on its shelf. The boots were underneath, side by side on a pile of old newspapers. Written inside, in marking ink, was a name; L. Wainwright. Erica picked them up gingerly, as if they were sacred relics. Perhaps they were Elsie's own boots, L for Lynden, left over from the days when he wrote poems on marrows, but they looked rather too new and shiny for that. She took off her trainers and socks and stood on the warm dry newspaper that Elsie had put down on the floor of the office.

'Chuck us a towel,' she called, and Elsie tossed in a handful of fairly clean rags. The Gremlin, seeing his advantage, instantly wound himself round Elsie's left leg, clinging with all four limbs and, by the looks of it, his teeth too. 'Bite him back,' Bunny crooned in an accurate and unkind imitation of Mrs Kermit. Erica dried her feet and first slid, then thrust, then drove them into the boots. They were much too tight against her damp skin and made her feel as though she were standing on tiptoe, but they were comfortingly dry. She rolled up her jeans until they just skimmed the tops of the boots and tittupped out to collect the Gremlin.

'Walkies!' Elsie said.

'Drownies,' said Bunny. 'Go and see the nice dentist.'

'Does he like going to the dentist?' Erica asked, as the Gremlin began to unwind himself from Elsie's leg.

'Like him? It's a horrid fascination,' Elsie said. 'He used to climb on a box and peer in, but the patients complained. That's why there's a curtain across the bottom of the window now. It happened to me once. Imagine it, lying there helpless with a mouth full of ironmongery and cotton wool and a jaw full of anaesthetic, and the Gremlin's face appears soundlessly at the window. I couldn't even scream.'

Erica held out her hand to the Gremlin and he followed her out, over the springing planks to the edge of the Black Lagoon, under the greasy sky.

'Over the Golden Gate,' Elsie sang out behind them.

'Oh, turn it up, Else, please. I wonder you haven't christened the compressor,' said Bunny.

This time when she rode home, there was no one standing in the road waiting for her, but Erica was sure, as she pedalled through the puddles, the ordinary normal-sized puddles at Calstead Corner, that there was going to be a row. There was no possible way of avoiding it except by turning the Iron Cow and cycling all the way to Norwich or by falling into the ditch and feigning death; and every turn of the pedals brought it closer. She had gone out in the rain when she had been told not to, she had stayed out until – she looked at her watch – after five, and she had wantonly exposed the Iron Cow to the dangers of rust.

The rain had stopped altogether now, so she had ridden home with the Jelly Mould dribbling through the wires of the freezer basket. Her jeans and trainers, dried in front of Elsie's paraffin heater, felt stiff, as if they belonged to someone else, but not so stiff as the boots that belonged to L. Wainwright. Because they were so small and she had worn them without socks, she had had to lie on the floor in the Cave while Elsie pulled them off for her. He had been so grateful to her for removing the Gremlin and exercising him round Polthorpe for an hour that he had asked her to come back on Monday; actually asked her, a real invitation.

'Three of us should be able to manage,' he had said. 'Two on the bikes and one on Gremlin detail. We'll take it in turns.' She still did not know who the boots belonged to.

She descended from the Iron Cow, crossed the road and

130

the gravel behind the house, walking and wheeling cautiously, to delay the row for a little while longer; but no one came out, even when she overturned a watering-can in the garage while hanging up the Jelly Mould.

Then, through a gap in the hedge, she saw Auntie Joan walking on the footpath, on her way home from cleaning the church. It suddenly occurred to Erica that quite possibly no one would have noticed that she had been out. Bending low, like an escaping pickpocket, she ran back across the gravel and in at the back door. The house was warm and quiet except for a distant murmur from the television. The living-room door was slightly ajar, just as she had left it, and when she pushed it noiselessly further open there were Uncle Peter and Robert on the settee, just as she had left them, and there were the athletes, still running round the track in the sunshine, only now the shadows were longer. Erica sat down silently at the table and looked at the screen. Even the green shape was where she had left it. The afternoon seemed to shrivel away as if it had never happened; the floods, the Gremlin, the boots, the Black Lagoon, the Golden Gate; all gone.

She heard Auntie Joan crossing the gravel like someone eating cornflakes with an open mouth, and the sound of the back-door handle turning. Howlett's Yard became very distant, a magical kingdom that you knew was there but that you could not get into simply by wanting, hidden behind a door in a wall that you could not always find. It was hard to believe, now she had left it, that it was still there; that Bunny and Elsie were still slopping about in the waters of the Black Lagoon, mending motor cycles, fending off the Gremlin.

The living-room door opened and Auntie Joan came in.

'Hullo,' Erica said. She would not normally have said anything, but she was feeling guilty and the worry was back, just under the belt of her jeans, and not moving, as if it were something that she had gulped down too quickly. Robert and Uncle Peter did not even turn their eyes from the television.

'Have you had a nice afternoon?' Auntie Joan asked, but not as if she wanted to know. 'Come on, Erica, and help me lay the tea.'

Erica followed her out, not minding at all that she had to help, but minding very much that Robert and Uncle Peter, who had done nothing at all all afternoon while Auntie Joan was working in the church, had not *offered* to help and had not been asked to. Robert, as far as she could see, had done nothing at all during the whole fortnight that she had been at Hall Farm Cottage, except to trap his finger in his own caterpillar snare. Ted's old boar, confined in his shed, led a more exciting life than Robert did.

The water in the dyke had risen so high during the floods that the Muscovy ducks returned and floated right in among the dwarf beans. They drifted about, bloated and lazy, scarcely bothering to stretch out their necks when they wanted a beakful. The peacock stayed away, perhaps afraid of getting its tail wet.

On Sunday the level had gone down. Erica looked at it from her window after waking from a dream in which she had been swimming in Elsie's Black Lagoon with a mouse and a frog which had also fallen in, while Panda, grown enormous and with her teeth very straight and businesslike, sat high above them on the Golden Gate Bridge and dipped at the water with a huge barbed paw.

When she arrived at the yard on Monday the waters there had gone down too, and the barrier had been removed from the mouth of the alley. She approached warily, looking out for the dangerous hole that Elsie had mentioned. All she found was a patch of white ash and cinders, so somebody must have filled it in. She wondered briefly if Elsie had managed to find a name for it before it was buried, if you could be said to bury a hole.

The Black Lagoon had gone back to being a puddle and the sandbag barrier had been dismantled, but the Golden

Gate was still there and on Pallet Island the Gremlin was sitting, with Panda.

'He's found something more interesting than us, at last,' Bunny said, as she entered the Cave.

'What's that?' Erica manhandled the table outside and unpacked her vegetables from the freezer basket.

'The island,' Bunny said. 'Elsie saw him prodding about on it so he gave him a can of coke and a bag of crisps, and told him he was shipwrecked. Looks like he believes it.'

Erica looked all round, but apart from Bunny the Cave was empty.

'Elsie likes children, doesn't he?'

'He must do,' Bunny said, shaking his head mournfully, as this only further confirmed his suspicion that Elsie had a screw loose, 'or he wouldn't have you here, would he,' he continued, tactlessly.

Erica threw down her carrots. 'That's different. He has me here to help with the bikes. You know he does. I *do* help.'

'If you say so.'

'I did that Fizzy, didn't I?'

'Oh yes, you earns your keep,' said Bunny. 'But Elsie's that soft he wouldn't have the heart to turn you out however useless you were. You should see him with his own two.'

'*Children!*'

'Nah, tortoises,' said Bunny.

'Tortoises?'

'Oh, wake up, Erica, do,' Bunny said. 'Of course I meant children.'

'I didn't know he was married.'

'That don't necessarily follow,' Bunny said, 'but he is.'

'I've never seen them.'

'They don't come here,' Bunny said, and something in his voice made Erica look up, quickly, but Bunny was bent over a Honda C70 which had been brought in coughing badly, late on Saturday afternoon. 'I took this for a spin before we opened up this morning. She won't do more than twenty in top, but she's ticking over O K. I reckon that's the points. If that is, you can do them – if you know how.'

Elsie came in and announced hollowly, 'We've been smitten by a plague of frogs.'

'He's always like this on Mondays,' Bunny said loudly, behind his hand. 'That's all that reading of the Bible on Sundays.'

'I read the Beano on Sundays,' Elsie said, 'and the Bible when I feel like it. Come and have a look.'

They went outside and round the corner to the dark cranny between Elsie's Cave and the side of the lavatories.

'And don't try using *them* today,' Elsie cautioned. 'There has been what is known in the trade as a blow-back. Owing to the high water table, I understand. No, actually, I don't understand, but you wouldn't get me in there for a considerable bribe this morning. Never mind; Yerbut has offered us facilities. Now, take a look at this.'

They stooped to see what he was pointing at. In the corner, where the grass was long, were frogs. They were coming, in a hurry, through a crack in the fencing and milling about round Elsie's feet. Erica tried to count, but there were too many, and they moved too fast.

'Don't tell the Gremlin,' Elsie said, 'or we'll have a frog-sticking party on our hands.'

'What are they doing?' Erica said.

'Just frogging about,' Bunny said. 'Right, Elsie, we've all had a look. Mind if we get back to work?'

'I only mentioned it,' Elsie said, as they returned to the Cave, 'because when I opened up the shop this morning and shifted the sandbags – while you were out on the Honda, Bunny – a couple hopped out past me and I found another under the Indian. They must be getting in at the back, somewhere.'

'Where've they come from?'

'I don't know. Apparently out of the sorting office, but it doesn't really seem likely. I suppose the rain flushed them out of somewhere and they drifted on the current.'

'How many frogs makes a plague?' Erica asked.

'One,' said Bunny.

'You haven't got a thing about frogs too, have you?' Elsie said, 'as well as spiders? Amphibiaphobia.'

'No, but I can do without them, any day of the week,' Bunny said. 'Come on, Erica, get that flywheel off and see what's doing inside. Elsie, Bill Hewitt's getting a bit urgent about his Yamaha. You wouldn't like to kind of *do* something to that, would you? Like mend it,' he said pointedly, but Elsie was off on a tack of his own.

'Say a hundred. I don't think we're at plague status yet. We can do a head count every morning. How many d'you think we've had so far, Erica? You were counting.'

'You said three.'

'Oh, that was in here. Still, I suppose we can only include them if they get in. What's three?'

'Too many,' Bunny said.

'An occurrence,' Elsie said. 'One to nine's an occurrence.' He was writing, small, square and black, on the back of an invoice. 'We've been smitten by an occurrence of frogs. Now, what about ten to twenty-nine?'

'An inconvenience,' Erica suggested.

'That's a good one. Thirty to forty-nine?'

'Look Else, just start that up, eh?' Bunny pleaded.

'Thirty to forty-nine's a nuisance.'

'That'd be a sight more than that,' Bunny said.

'Over fifty's a damn nuisance, and over eighty is a plague.' He pinned his paper on the door of the office, wrote on it *Monday* and put a tick beside *Occurrence*.

'I'll do the counting,' Erica said.

'No cheating,' Elsie said. 'Stick to the rules. If it's seventy-nine, it's still only a damn nuisance. We need eighty for a plague.'

'I reckon you two actually want a plague,' Bunny said, disgustedly.

'It's all part of life's rich pattern. There aren't many people who can say they've been smitten by a plague of frogs,' Elsie said, and finally turned his attention to the Yamaha.

'If you did that with customers,' Bunny said, 'I could see some sense in it.'

'A plague of customers,' Elsie said, and leaned on the saddle, looking round at his Cave. 'Now that would be worth having.'

Chapter Sixteen

'You got those points available yet, Erica?' Bunny said.

'I've just got to adjust them,' Erica said. 'I've locked the flywheel.'

'Yes, well, you leave that be,' Bunny said, advancing upon the C70. 'I'll adjust them. Did you time yourself?'

'Fifteen minutes so far.'

'Plus five either end for me ... twenty-five ... call it thirty ... that'll be three quid when he comes in. Note that down.'

'Hark, hark, the frogs do bark, the beggars are coming to town,' Elsie chanted, down behind the Indian. 'Here's another one. How many's that, Erica?'

Erica did some more calculations. 'Eleven.'

'What did we say eleven would be? Where *are* they coming from? I can't find a gap.'

Erica consulted the chart that Elsie had tacked up earlier. 'That's an inconvenience now – there's another, in the doorway.'

'I've been smitten by an inconvenience of Wainwrights,' Bunny said, adjusting the points through the hole in the flywheel as Yerbut came in. 'I've got the Wainwrights something chronic.'

'Wainwritis,' Elsie said helpfully, without rancour. 'Erica, that's no frog, that's Yerbut.'

'Yer, but there's frogs all over the place out here,' Yerbut said. 'Swimming in the puddle and all.'

'Oh, where?' Erica said, remembering her dream and then wondering if she had dreamed it after all and had instead just that moment thought of it. She went out into the yard, leaving Elsie and Yerbut to examine the works wireless that Yerbut had brought back. The frogs were not alone. Panda had come across the Golden Gate Bridge and was wandering among them, peering dimly but delightedly at so much lunch leaping about. When she found a frog that would keep still long enough for her to home in on it, she sat down heavily, like an old lady worn out by a shopping expedition, and began to pat it. The frog put its hands over its eyes and froze. Panda tried to turn it over and the frog became very flat. Erica lifted Panda away and she immediately sank to the bottom of her skin, leaving her fur like a half-empty bag in Erica's hands. Erica put her down on the far side of the Black Lagoon, knowing that it would take her a long time to walk back round it, and took the frog to Elsie. It lay motionless on her palm like a little cold model of a frog.

'Has she killed it? What shall I do?'

'Put it back in the puddle and it'll swell up again,' Elsie said. Erica went to administer First Aid to the victim, and after a few minutes, as Elsie had predicted, it reflated and began to flap about nervously, but by this time Panda had found another frog and was lazily paddling it as if she were shaping dough. Her tail twitched and her false teeth flashed, but she was so old that her claws would not come out and after a bit she moved away to find a third frog, leaving the other to recover on its own.

Rescuing frogs from Panda could turn out to be one of those never-ending jobs like painting the Forth Bridge. Erica

138

left her to it and went back into the cave to polish the Indian's headlight. She made herself a throne of newspapers and was settling down to work when she heard the entirely unexpected sound of high heels crossing the Golden Gate. She looked up and saw a lady walking fastidiously across the Black Lagoon, and a girl, a little younger than Erica, or smaller at any rate, following with great care. They were both elegantly shod and the lady was wearing a pretty summer frock, looking like a rose in a coalhole in those surroundings. The girl wore a pale green cat-suit. Behind them, on the far side of the Lagoon, Erica saw a white perambulator, dashingly streamlined like a long-distance coach, with a clean baby in it. It seemed highly unlikely that they had come to inquire about motor cycles; maybe the fame of the vegetables had spread. She stood up, wiping her hands professionally on a rag that was far dirtier than her hands were, and went out to stand by the table.

'Good morning,' Erica said, and laid her hand invitingly on a pile of beetroot. They both looked at her as if they could not for the life of them imagine what she was doing there, and came down off the Golden Gate, walking past her into the Cave. Erica hardly liked to follow them in, but she listened hard and heard Bunny say cautiously, 'Hello, Sharon. Hello, Lucy.'

'Hello, Bernard, where's Lynden?' the lady said, and there was a clattering sound as Elsie rose from behind a pile of something and overturned it. Erica, startled to hear him addressed by his real name, which scarcely seemed real since she so seldom heard it, looked round the edge of the door frame. On the other side, staring back at her, was the girl in the pale green cat-suit. They gazed at each other for several seconds until the girl said, 'Seen enough?'

There were plenty of answers to that, but Erica could not think of any of them. The girl went on staring, until her mother called, 'Lucy! Come in here, out of that mud!'

Lucy made a really disagreeable face and trotted inside.

139

Her behind was too wide for the cat-suit, Erica noted. She went over and stood with Elsie and the lady. Elsie put out his hand. Lucy jerked away and said, 'Oh, don't, Dad – you'll get oil all over me.'

Dad. *Dad?*

It was Elsie's family.

'Who's that?' Lucy said, as if Erica were not there at all. 'What's *she* doing here?'

'That's my new mechanic,' Elsie said. 'This is Erica.'

'I should have thought,' Mrs Wainwright said, and not bothering to lower her voice, 'that you had enough to do without letting the place fill up with other people's kids.'

'She keeps young Gordon out, at any rate,' Elsie said, only he was Lynden now, Mr Wainwright, and no one had handles any more.

'We're going to Yarmouth,' Mrs Wainwright said. 'Mum rang up. She's got to go to hospital again this afternoon, and she wants me to go with her.'

'What about Lucy?' Elsie said.

'She'll come too.'

'She won't want to sit in the waiting-room all afternoon. Why don't you leave her here?' Elsie said, hopefully.

'They don't keep you long.'

Elsie persisted. 'D'you want to stop here, Lucy?'

Lucy said nothing, but she looked down the whole length of her pale green cat-suit to the green suede trainers at the end of either leg. She had found a raft of newspaper to stand on to keep them clean. Erica, over the welts in mud, found herself hoping very much that Lucy was not going to stay and thinking that Elsie looked rather different as somebody's father. Bunny – Bernard – stood solemnly in the background.

'No, she's coming with me,' Mrs Wainwright said. 'What on earth is that terrible smell?'

'The drains,' Elsie said. 'Howlett's are supposed to be getting them seen to, but you know what they're like.'

'And you expect me to leave Lucy here ... ? I don't know when we'll be back. There's plenty of stuff in the freezer.'

'Erica can run across and get us sausage rolls,' Elsie said.

'Well, I can't stop,' said Mrs Wainwright, but she did not go and Lucy just stood there glaring at Erica and gnawing the strap of her little red shoulder-bag. No one said anything and Erica felt as she had once done at home when she was sitting in the dark, thinking, and Mum had come in suddenly and switched all the lights on. The Cave was just a run-down repair shop, Bunny was Bernard, too fat in his boilersuit, and Elsie was only a man whose wife was angry with him. Erica did not know why she was angry and did not know what to think, and for the first time in weeks wished herself safely back in Calstead at Hall Farm Cottage.

'Keep the flag flying,' Elsie said to Erica, and walked with his family over the Golden Gate, over the planks. Panda, bored with frogs, lurched after them and tried to rub against various ankles. Lucy side-stepped, and although she was nearly on dry land again, slipped from the plank and stood heavily on one immaculate shoe in the ooze on the shore of the Black Lagoon; the big puddle.

Mrs Wainwright turned furiously upon Elsie. 'Now look what's happened!' Erica knew that she meant 'Now look what you've done,' although Elsie had not done anything.

'Oh, come off it,' Elsie protested mildly. 'It's only mud. Wait till it dries and it'll brush off.'

'That's *oil!*' Mrs Wainwright yelled. It really was a yell. Lucy was hopping about, her hair bouncing on her shoulders and her bag bouncing on her hip. Erica, standing in the mouth of the Cave beside Bunny, saw what it meant to be dancing with rage.

'Now she'll have to go home and change. We'll be late,' Mrs Wainwright was saying, not shouting but in an angry, carrying hiss, like the air line.

'Hang about,' said Elsie, in a flat spin, 'I've got her boots in here. She left them at Easter – bring them out will you, Erica?'

141

She had actually worn Lucy's boots. She fetched them from the office and ran across the plank bridge to where Lucy was standing on one leg, while her mother supported her, as if she had been dangerously injured instead of having just stepped in the mud. Lucy set up a fresh howl.

'They're all filthy! Someone's been wearing them!'

'I only lent them to Erica when we were flooded,' Elsie said. 'Come on, don't be soft, Lucy. You won't catch anything from Erica.'

Erica stood on the end of the plank with a boot in either hand. Lucy snatched them from her and threw them, with unexpected accuracy, into the middle of the puddle. Then she began to scream in earnest, and the baby joined in. There was nothing that Erica could do; or Elsie, come to that. He stood and watched his daughter throwing a fit in the middle of the yard while Mrs Wainwright mobbed him. She was speaking quite loudly now, but nothing could be heard above Lucy's siren screams. Erica scrambled back across the planks, wrestled the bicycle out of the fireweed and ran it across the shore of the puddle. By the time she had reached the family group she had gathered too much momentum to stop, or slow down, or change direction, but she could see what was going to happen. As they all jumped out of the way a great bow wave of inky spray broke on either side of the front wheel, at the moment she was levering herself into the saddle. Elsie's unlooked-for grin was the last thing she saw as she plunged into the mouth of the alley, but she left behind her an awful silence. Whatever had happened had stopped even Lucy screaming.

She went out to look at the marrows after tea. The peacock was there already, strutting and pecking, but Robert was down in the dyke after the Muscovy ducks. Erica slipped beneath the branches of the Bramley to where the airborn marrow now hung like a dirigible from its mooring mast. She moved the leaves and parted the long grass. During the wet weekend the marrows had grown apace, and the rinds had

142

split where, last time she had looked, there had been only scratches. ROBERT IS A FAT TWIT had come on the most although VOTE LABOUR, which having fewer letters than the rest was written larger, was the more eye-catching. Erica covered them all up, very carefully, before going to help clear away the stall.

Already the evenings were growing darker, and there were stars showing in the east. That night Ted forgot to turn off the gas gun in his pea field beyond the pigsties and an explosion woke Erica at dawn. She looked out of the window towards the coast, and over the dunes Orion hung, low in the sky, the winter constellation. It was the thirtieth of August. Summer was almost over, autumn was coming and in a few days she would be going back to Norwich, leaving Elsie in his Cave, in his kingdom, with his boot-faced Lucy.

Chapter Seventeen

'Well,' said Auntie Joan, on Tuesday towards lunchtime, 'aren't you going into Polthorpe today?'

'I don't go *every* day,' Erica said. 'I mean, they don't expect me *every* day.'

'I shouldn't think they'd *want* you every day,' Robert remarked. Erica doubted if he even knew where she went.

'We could do with getting rid of some of them beans,' Auntie Joan said. 'And I can't pick the marrows fast enough. Perhaps you could pop in after lunch.'

It was impossible to pop anywhere on the Iron Cow, but Auntie Joan made it sound as simple as crossing the kitchen. When Erica had wanted to go to Polthorpe she had tried to stop her, and now that Erica did not want to go she tried to persuade her; but that thought was not really reasonable, for Auntie Joan could not know that Erica now actively feared the thought of going back to Elsie's kingdom to encounter angry Mrs Wainwright and shrieking Lucy. She was not sure any more that Elsie had been grinning as she cycled wildly through the puddle.

Supposing Mrs Wainwright and Lucy had asked about her

when she was gone? Had Elsie shrugged and said that she was no one in particular, or had he explained that she was good for tappet clearances and helped him with the frog count, and that they were in partnership over the vegetable stall? She wondered if Bunny had put in a good word for her. Bunny had not sounded very enthusiastic that time he had told her about Elsie having children. She'd not even seen the baby properly.

'Well,' Auntie Joan said, breaking in on her thoughts, 'at least you ought to go and say good-bye.'

'Good-bye?'

'Well, you'll be going home in a few days, won't you? School start next week. I were going to ring Anne this afternoon. To see when she expect you back.'

Erica had not thought of going quite so soon. She remembered guiltily that she had never sent Yob his card, and then she had a sudden picture of Auntie Joan, or Uncle Peter, or Robert, strolling under the apple trees one evening in the cool of the day and coming across the marrows, the huge unavoidable marrows, shouting COME TO SUNNY CALSTEAD, ELSIE WAINWRIGHT RULES OK?, VOTE LABOUR, ROBERT IS A FAT TWIT. She would have to destroy the evidence, and she hardly knew which was worse; fearing that Robert would see his personalized marrow or knowing that Elsie would never see his; and where on earth could she put them?

That afternoon, when Auntie Joan had gone to telephone from the callbox at Calstead Corner and Robert was busy trying to trap something, possibly a stone, she went down to the marrows and uncovered her secret messages. The marrows had grown alarmingly, and now it was only too clear what she had written. Regretfully she decided that there was a chance she could smuggle out Elsie's marrow and ERICA TIMPERLEY WAS HERE, but the rest would have to go. It might be possible to drown them in the dyke – or would they float? She had forgotten how spiny the stems were and had never known how difficult it could be to detach a marrow from its stalk without leaving a scar. She wrapped her fingers in a fold of her sweater and twisted until the great solid balloons rolled away free into the grass, then carried them round the lawn by a circuitous route between the raspberry canes and poked them through the hedge. She heard them roll into the dock leaves at the bottom of the ditch on the other side.

When she returned to the Bramley she found that she had been only just in time to save the two marrows and was not, definitely not, in time to hide the others. Robert had arrived with his cat-trap netting and was standing there, staring, mouth open. He was staring downwards, into the grass.

Erica had doubted sometimes if he could read – he did not seem to be able to follow the sports results on television without the commentary – but there was no doubt about it now. With surprising speed he began foraging in the long grass, uncovering marrow after incriminating marrow: BAN THE BOMB, MERCURY MOTOR CYCLES, COME TO SUNNY CALSTEAD FOR YOUR HOLIDAY, VOTE LABOUR. Robert saw her and straightened up.

'Did you done this?'

'That was the peacock,' Erica said.

'You've writ on our marrows,' Robert insisted. She was almost surprised that he had not believed her. Everything about him seemed round: eyes, mouth, face. He was not impressed, he was outraged. 'What you do that for?'

'You do that with a pin, when they're ever so small,' Erica said, in the wan hope that he might be interested and want to try it for himself. 'And when they grow, the letters get bigger. I've got a good long pin if you want to have a go.'

'You're barmy!' Robert exploded suddenly. 'You're raving barmy. What you want to do that for? *We won't be able to sell them now!*'

Erica could see, as he could not, ROBERT IS A FAT TWIT skulking under a particularly large leaf. She pointed hurriedly to BAN THE BOMB, which lay beside him.

146

'I bet you could sell them if you put them out on the stall. I mean, you could put that one in the back window of a car, instead of a sticker.'

Robert glared at it. 'Ban the Bomb? What bomb?'

'That bomb!' Erica yelled in despair and disgust, and swung the aerial marrow against his head. He staggered back, onto ROBERT IS A FAT TWIT, uncovering it utterly, and so the worst of her sins was exposed.

It had never struck her before, but Auntie Joan, Uncle Peter and Robert were very like three marrows themselves: three raving, slavering marrows with teeth and hair and enormous voices that went on and on crying the same thing, like the peacock: 'Whyyyyyyyyy?'

'I thought that was funny.' Erica had lost count of the times she had said it. It would not make any difference if she went on saying it until bedtime, which looked like being earlier than usual tonight. No one took any notice. They could not see that finding something funny might seem a good reason for doing it – at the time. Erica felt that none of them, at any time in their lives, had ever found anything funny; now that she came to think of it, she could not remember ever hearing them laugh, except at a proper joke, the kind that came in a sort of frame with a label on it that said JOKE in case you didn't notice what it was. Nor could they understand that saying the same thing over and over again was not going to make her any sorrier than she was already.

They would never understand what a good idea it had seemed in Elsie's Cave by the Black Lagoon, but then they would never understand Elsie anyway. They would think he was mad and ought to be put away. The only thing that kept her there in the kitchen, answering the question about once every three minutes and hearing a catalogue of all her old crimes committed over the last three weeks, including going out on Saturday against orders (Auntie Joan had found the oilskin still wet and had sneakily said nothing), was the noble thought that she must not reveal the identity of the person who had given her the idea and thus basely betray Elsie. Uncle Peter might go round there and squash him flat with one massive swipe, as Panda had flattened the frogs. He was several times larger than Elsie, upwards and outwards.

Thinking of Panda and the frogs, just for that tiny moment, made her smile.

'Out!' Auntie Joan said suddenly. 'I don't know why we bother talking. You hent even listening. Go on. Go away. Out.'

Erica went, a little stunned. She had expected to be sent to bed, or at least upstairs, or threatened with deprivation of tea. Just being told to go away was much worse, as if it no longer mattered – and no one would care – what became of her once she had gone. Robert was blocking the doorway to the hall and the stairs. She opened the back door instead and went out onto the gravel.

There was a pound in her pocket and it was twenty past five. If she took off now, without stopping to pack – or to rescue the hidden marrows from the ditch – she could run to Calstead Corner and catch the bus home, back to Norwich. Mum would be furious, but at least she could explain to Mum, and Dad could drive out in the car to collect her clothes and say sorry properly. Coming to it fresh, he *would* be sorry. She turned on her heel and headed for the road. Even if anyone were watching from the kitchen they would never catch her up; even if Auntie Joan leaped onto the Iron Cow and pursued her she would still reach the bus-stop first, and if the bus were late she would run up the lane towards the Methodist Chapel and flag it down when it came into sight. That was the one good thing about living in the country: the buses stopped where you wanted them to.

She was sure that the distant flicker of red between the willows on the Tokesby road must be the bus making its winding way towards the Happing Turn at Calstead Corner, but as she came out onto the roadway and got ready to run, Ted Hales called to her from the other side of his thorn hedge.

148

Erica waved, because it would have been rude not to – poor Ted had nothing to do with marrows, and because of them she had nearly cut him dead last time they met – and would have hurried on, but Ted waved back and called out 'Good afternoon!' Erica had to answer him, although the bus was already at Iken Fen, stopping to let someone get on, and this meant turning her head. Ted was digging over by the hen-run and the little private hut where the young sow had farrowed. He put down his spade and came towards her. She could not run on, pretending that she had not seen, and leave Ted to walk across his plot to talk to someone who would no longer be there when he arrived.

Ted came up level with her on the far side of the hedge. 'My old lady died last night,' he said.

Erica looked to where he was pointing. Among the bind-weed and fat hen-plants a bulky shape, under a tarpaulin, lay near to Ted's maternity ward. Ted was obviously digging a grave. Surely it wasn't for Mrs Hales?

'My old sow,' said Ted. He looked again at the bulge. Erica looked at Ted. Clearly he could not have felt worse if it *had* been Mrs Hales who had passed on.

'What did she die of?'

'Old age. She knew,' Ted said. He leaned on his spade. 'She knew she were going last night, and I knew. I tried to get her to move round to the straw stack, but she wouldn't go. Just laid down where she was. And then she died.'

'Why did you want to get her round to the straw stack?' Erica asked. 'Is that more comfortable?'

'Ground's softer,' Ted explained, practically. 'That's like concrete over there, where she went. Poor old girl. I've been digging that hole all afternoon, and that's still only three feet down, and she're swelling all the time.' He looked regretfully over his shoulder at the recumbent bulge.

'How much does she weigh?'

'Several hundredweight. I've had her from a gilt. Poor old girl.'

Together they observed a short silence in honour of the deceased. Erica was very glad that the deceased was not Mr Davis, Ted's old boar. That really would have cut him up. Out of the tail of her eye Erica saw the bus pause at Calstead Corner, shudder and move on.

Slowly she went back to the house. There was no one indoors; they were all down the garden, under the apple trees, apparently holding a wake for the marrows. Perhaps they had died of their injuries and Uncle Peter was even now digging a grave for them as Ted was digging one for his old lady. Erica crept upstairs and thought of the bus, the 705, swaying empty along the empty lanes towards the main road and Norwich. It would be past Polthorpe by now, past the coal yard, the Broad and the sewage works, heading for Wroxham, the final frontier. If it hadn't been for Ted's old lady she might have been on it, almost halfway home – well, almost halfway to halfway home.

She sat on the bed, looking out of the window, and began to feel glad that she had missed the bus by stopping to talk to Ted; not glad that she had missed the bus, but glad that she had stopped.

She no longer felt so guilty about the marrows and all the other things that, so she had suddenly discovered, she was supposed to have done; like cheeking Auntie Joan and teasing Robert and telling lies and associating with unrespectable people – which must be Elsie. She was not all bad after all. She had stopped to talk to Ted, at the cost of her own comfort. She felt virtuous and kind, and anyway, she was sure, Elsie would have done the same.

Chapter Eighteen

Marrows were not mentioned next morning, and Auntie Joan was distant but polite. Erica saw the marrows on the compost heap when she went to open the greenhouse and put up the peacock trap, stacked obtrusively one upon the other on the very summit of the heap, a monument to conspicuous waste. She looked away from it and hurried on.

It was difficult laying out the stall after breakfast as though nothing had happened, because Auntie Joan would insist on behaving as though nothing had happened, which made what had happened seem a lot worse than it had been. They laid out onions, turnips, swedes, carrots and beetroot, but there were no marrows. No one mentioned marrows.

After they had finished and the bell was in position, Erica said, 'Can I borrow the bike to go into Polthorpe, please?'

'No,' said Auntie Joan, quite pleasantly. 'I'll need that to go down to Calstead Corner to ring your mother.' She did not even call her Anne now. 'To tell her you'll be going home tomorrow instead. I think that're best, don't you?'

Erica thought that it was the best thing that she had heard in a long time, until she remembered that she would be going

151

home in disgrace, and that unless she went into Polthorpe today, on foot if necessary, she would not get the chance to say good-bye to Bunny and Elsie. She could tell that she would not be allowed out on the Iron Cow, even after Auntie Joan had finished with it. She would have to go on foot, or on the bus, and there were the secret marrows to consider.

On the back of the kitchen door, among the hot water bottles, hung various bags and baskets; tote bags, shopping bags, carrier bags and a big wicker basket that fell down at intervals into the sink. They all had a special purpose; you probably had to fill out a form in triplicate if you wanted to use one, even for the right purpose, and probably none of them was meant for carrying marrows. However, she took down a big plastic carrier, crept out and retrieved the marrows from their bolthole in the ditch by the road. During the night fat slugs had come to browse. There were several stuck to the undersides, and ERICA TIMPERLEY WAS HERE had been slightly nibbled. She peeled away the slugs, put the marrows into the bag and put the bag back into the ditch, where it lay disguised as litter thrown out by a careless motorist, waiting to be collected later.

The yard was empty, the puddle had dried up and the plank bridge had been disassembled. Not a frog was in sight; only, in the distance, the Gremlin could be seen, clambering about in Bill Birdcycle's wrecked van that was going to become a television star; but he was too busy prodding to notice her.

From the shop she heard the thud of the compressor. She looked in, feeling that all this had happened before, and there was Elsie, welding, just as he had been on the day when she first saw him. In the corner behind the Indian, Bunny moved about, bent low, a huge uncertain shape in the gloom.

'What can I do you for?' Elsie said, when he saw her, just as he had done the first time. Then he said, 'Ah, it's you.'

'I've come to say good-bye,' Erica said. 'I'm going home tomorrow.'

'That's a bit sudden, isn't it?' Elsie said.

'We had a sort of row.' Erica decided not to tell him what the row had been about in case he felt guilty about having suggested the cause of it. 'But I'd have had to go back soon anyway. School starts next week.'

'So does Lucy's, now I come to think of it,' Elsie said. 'So does the Gremlin's.' He brightened momentarily, but he was looking towards the back of the shop. In the office, on the high stool, legs dangling, sat Lucy Wainwright, scowling at Erica through the glass with all the spare skin on her forehead squeezed into lumps and ridges between her eyebrows. She was dressed for work in a pair of exquisitely clean dungarees which were tucked into the tops of the boots that Erica had borrowed, shining clean again and no doubt fumigated.

'Come and say hello,' Elsie invited her, but Lucy turned her shoulder and looked the other way at the open door and, since it was hanging on a level with her eyes, at the frog count.

'Did we ever get to a plague?' Erica asked.

'Not even as far as a damn nuisance,' Elsie said, regretfully.

'*One* frog is a damn nuisance,' Bunny reiterated, from behind the Indian. Since she had last seen it it had regained its forks, as well as its front and rear wheels. Bunny was at work on the engine. It was hard to accept that now she would never see it restored to its full glory.

Lucy said very clearly from the office, 'I got Dad to throw them out. The frogs. They made me feel all eugh!'

'Amphibiaphobia,' Elsie said. He looked embarrassed.

They stood silently for a few moments.

'I brought you a present,' Erica said, reaching into the carrier bag. 'They aren't really big enough yet, but if I'd left them in the garden you'd never have seen them.' She brought out ERICA TIMPERLEY WAS HERE and ELSIE WAINWRIGHT RULES OK? and passed them to him. Elsie held one in each hand.

'Lovely workmanship,' he said. 'Just right as they are. They'd have looked very vulgar if they'd got any bigger; gross. Just what I wanted.' He placed one on either end of the bench. 'Come and look at this, Lucy.'

Lucy slid down from her stool and came out of the office, stepping carefully in her glossy boots. She stared at the marrows and then at Erica.

'I think that's silly,' she said.

Elsie never knew when to give up.

'We've still got some little ones at home, behind the shed. You could do a couple for Harvest Festival.'

Lucy shrugged and went back into the office, where she sat on her little stool and gazed blankly at the place where Erica was standing, but not at her. Once again, nobody said anything.

A motor cycle was heard in the alleyway. Elsie went outside, as he'd never done before, to see who was coming. Lucy reached out and closed the door of the office so that she sat inside the glass walls like a creature in a vivarium on a school window-sill. Erica went over to the Indian.

'Why's she here?'

'Why d'you think?' Bunny said. 'That's exactly what she said about you on Monday. "Who's *she*? What's *she* doing here?"'

'But she never came before.'

'She's here because you're here, or because she thought you might be,' Bunny said. 'Same as yesterday. You're telling me she never came before. Can't be too soon for me before she goes away again. Talk about Big Brother watching you.'

'She's never come to see *me*,' Erica protested. 'She doesn't like me.'

'She doesn't like anybody, that one,' Bunny said, 'and she doesn't like getting dirty. And her mum doesn't like her getting dirty either, but when she saw you here the other day she thought she was missing something. She's been like that ever since she was a little kid.'

154

Erica looked at Lucy in the office, glassed over, afraid of missing something, missing everything. Bunny looked at Erica through the skeleton of the Indian.

'She's jealous.'

'Jealous of me?'

'Of course she is. Here you are, having a high old time with her dad, *her* dad, remember, up to your eyebrows in grease and muck, counting frogs and giving everything daft names, and where's she? Stuck at home, that's where, keeping her shoes clean and minding the baby. Wouldn't you be jealous?'

'But I wouldn't stay at home.'

'Yes, well, maybe she won't any more. We've all got our crosses to bear,' Bunny said. 'She's mine. Still, it's made her old man very happy having her here. Can't think why. I don't know what her mum'll have to say about that, though.'

'Does she mind?'

'Who d'you think dresses Lucy up like a Sindy doll and has high strikes if she gets mud on her socks?' Bunny waved his spanner. 'She never wanted Else to go into bikes anyway. She still thinks that if she keeps mobbing him he'll go back to what he was trained for. Nice and respectable. Clean. Pays well,' Bunny said. 'There's no money in bikes. Less every day.'

Elsie came back from dealing with his customer.

'Sorry about that,' he said. 'Now, where were we – oh, yes – saying good-bye.'

'Thank you for having me,' Erica said. 'I enjoyed it.' It was like leaving a party. 'Can I come back and see you sometime?'

'Of course you can. You'll be staying at Calstead again, won't you?'

'I don't think so,' Erica said. 'But I could come out specially on the bus – if I wouldn't be in the way.'

'In the way?'

'Well ...' Erica, without meaning to, looked past him at Lucy in her glass case.

'You mean, this place isn't big enough for both of you?' Elsie said. 'I don't think you need worry about that. She'll never make a mechanic; not like you. You've got the feeling for it. You are *going* to be a mechanic, aren't you?'

Erica nodded.

'Well, there's always a job for you here. If I can ever afford an apprentice, I'll take you on. Shake on it.'

They shook hands.

'I've got the marrows to remember you by,' Elsie said. 'They'll last the winter, with care. Good-bye, Erica Timperley, who was here.'

'I never did get a handle,' Erica said.

'Well, you did,' said Elsie, 'but it was such a mouthful I never used it. Good-bye, Eroica Symphony.'

'What's that?'

'Music by Beethoven, haven't you heard of it?'

'No.'

'You've heard of *him?*'

'Yes.'

'That's all right then.' He hummed a few notes.

'And that's my handle?'

'It is here.'

Erica said good-bye to Bunny, and they shook hands across the Indian. 'Come back and see her when she's finished. She's going to the museum at Yarmouth, after. She's been booked in advance.'

'Let me know if you ever see another one,' Elsie said, as she went out of the door. 'I shall kind of miss this one when it's gone.' As she entered the alley he came to the door and yelled, 'I never did find those jump leads!'

She caught the first bus out on Friday. As usual the whole length of Polthorpe Street was clogged with traffic, owing to a van parked askew outside the Co-op and a breakdown at the far end near the coal yard. Erica sat on the top deck, looking down at Polthorpe from a new angle, and she would have missed seeing the mouth of the alley if the bus had not been halted for the fourth time outside Marsh's Service Station. The alley was just opposite her window and she looked along it. As if through a telescope she saw the Gremlin prodding in the distance, and Panda searching for frogs, while down below Bunny looked hurriedly at his watch as he turned the corner and scuttled massively down the alley. She looked for Elsie, and did not see him. He must be already in his shop, already at work; it was all going on without her, and always would, unless she could get back again. She pressed her face to the window as if staring would make seeing easier. The bus started suddenly and she looked up, just in time to read the topmost sign of the row on the wall, one that she had never noticed before; MERCURY MOTOR CYCLES. PROPRIETOR, L. C. WAINWRIGHT; and then the bus moved on.

GLOSSARY

BAST	Also called bass and raffia. Fiber from inner bark of trees, used for tying up plants.
BEANO	Weekly comic strip paper of lively vulgarity. *Everyone* reads it, or has read it.
BIRO	Ballpoint pen.
BOILER-SUIT	Overalls with jacket and trousers made as one garment.
CALABRESE	Variety of sprouting broccoli. (Calabrian)
CARRIER BAG	Plastic bag sold or given away in stores with the name of the store on the side.
CAT-SUIT	Jumpsuit.
CHAD	A drawing of a head looking over a wall (it often appeared on walls) complaining about shortages, especially during World War II. e.g., "Wot, no soap?" (Similar to Kilroy at the same time in the U.S.)
CHAIRS AREN'T AT HOME	Used of someone who is mentally unsound, but not actually insane. Elsie has a collection of such phrases, e.g., Out of his tree.

CHIPPY	Takeout shop selling fish and chips (French fries).
CLANGER	To drop a clanger is to make a tactless error out loud.
COURGETTE	Zucchini squash.
DRIFTS	Tools for making or enlarging holes in metal. In this case, the drift would be used for knocking out a damaged bush, which is the lining of an axle-hole.
FAG ENDS	Cigarette butts.
FAIRINGS	Streamlining panels on the fronts of motorcycles.
FLOG	Sell.
GAFFER	Usually a foreman. In this case, the manager, and Erica's mum is putting him down. He wouldn't call himself the gaffer.
GAS GUN	Small cannon left in fields, especially of crops such as peas or beans, that can be preset to fire at intervals in order to scare birds. It does not fire bullets, but makes a very loud report. It is fueled by a cylinder of compressed gas, usually butane.
GELIGNITE	Explosive based on blasting-gelatin, a nitroglycerine solution.
GUNGE	Greasy deposits of oil and dirt.
HIGH STRIKES	Hysterics.
HOOVERING	Using a vacuum cleaner, regardless of the make.
LOKE	This word is used only in Norfolk. It means a lane with a dead end.
LOO	Toilet/bathroom, but not a bathroom without a toilet in it. 'Bathroom' is a room with a bathtub or shower in it.
LORRY	Truck.

MARROWS	Squashes.
M.O.T.	Ministry of Transport. The government department that deals with roads and vehicles. The M.O.T. test imposes a standard of roadworthiness on cars (or, in this case, motorcycles) over a certain age.
NATIONAL GRID	System of relaying electrical current around the British Isles.
NOBBLE	Interfere with.
ON THE LATCH	A door with a lock that is fixed at 'open' so that the door can be closed without actually locking.
PAINTING THE FORTH BRIDGE	Long iron railway bridge over the Firth (estuary) of Forth in Scotland. It takes so long to paint it that when the painters have finished at one end, they have to begin again immediately at the other. Hence, a job that is never finished.
PEGS	Clothespins.
PELICAN CROSSINGS	Pedestrian street crossings with traffic signals.
REGULO 6	A regulo is the dial on a gas oven for setting the temperature. Regulo 6 equals about 350 degrees Fahrenheit.
ROUNDERS BATS	Rounders is a game similar to, but much gentler than, baseball and is played in most English junior/grade schools. The bat is like a baseball bat, but shorter and lighter.
SECATEURS	Pruning shears.
SPANNERS	Wrenches. In England, a 'wrench' is an adjustable spanner.
STAITHE	Place where boats moor on inland waterways.
SWARFEGA	Industrial cleanser in the form of green jelly used for removing oil from the skin.

SWEDES	Variety of turnip (Swedish).
TAPPET	Part of an internal combustion engine.
TITTUPPED	Walked mincingly.
TRAINERS	Running shoes. These can be the shoes that runners and joggers use, but usually they are inexpensive imitations, for children and teenagers.
TROLLEY	Shopping cart.
TRUG	Shallow rectangular gardening basket with rounded corners, usually made of bent wood.
TYRE LEVERS	Metal levers used for removing tires from bicycle wheels before repairing punctures.
WORKS WIRELESS	One of Elsie's handles. A factory, mill, or plant is known as a 'works' by the people who live near it or have jobs there. (e.g., steel works, gas works) You wouldn't say it of a power station, though, and Elsie's shop is much too small to be a real works. Wireless (transmission of signals by electromagnetic waves, not by wire) is our old word for a radio. Very few people use it now, but Elsie's radio is very ancient.